PRECARIOUS
WATERS

AND OTHER DARK TALES

PAMELA JEFFS

For Piper and Dakota.

Reviews

Lush in detail and fierce with retribution, *Precarious Waters* is a spellbinding collection that should be on the must-read list for anyone who loves dark speculative fiction with heart. From selkies, to Furies, to re-animated dead and more, Pamela Jeffs draws on mythologies old and new to tell tales that are as beautifully ominous as they are powerfully redemptive. Vividly imagined worlds, characters and conflicts hook you from the very first line to the satisfying last. Get on board. You're in for an emotional rollercoaster ride.

Geneve Flynn, Shirley Jackson, Aurealis, and two-time Bram Stoker award-winning author, editor, and poet

CONTENTS

Precarious Waters 7

Dread Circus 18

Monstrous In Nature 28

Universe, Devoured 45

Origins and Assembly 63

Passenger 84

These Many Dead Men 106

Patchwork Reapers 124

All Who Are Warriors 141

Acknowledgments 158

References 159

About the Author 160

Other Titles 161

Precarious Waters

Just before dawn, when they say the night is darkest, the sea still shines. Waves, laced with phosphorescence, lap the quiet shore and a pale-faced moon, bejewelled in her collar of stars, smiles down. The cliffs loom dark behind me, rising salt-slick and razor-edged. Above them a small fishing village slumbers. At this hour, only the quiet voices of the first fishermen are heard, readying their boats for a morning on the water.

I should leave.

I'll be the one they hunt if they see me.

For in these parts, a selkie bride is a prize men would die for.

But the promise of a dawn soon to break keeps me. It can't hurt to linger a few moments more. I recline against a pile of rocks whose stout feet soak in the surf. My belly presses tight to my ribs, full from a night of feeding and I am at ease with the world. I twist my fingers through the fur edge of the rich, sable-coloured sea dress that lies across my knees. Yes. Just a few more minutes and then I'll return to my seal form and to the sea.

I close my eyes, letting the music of the waves lull me.

It is a full sun climbing toward the ninth hour that draws me to wakefulness—that and the faint rumble of diesel engines carried on a crisp sea breeze. I curse my carelessness and scramble, drawing my sea dress across my shoulders. The fur-skin fabric clings and beneath it, my muscles shift and bones click. My true shape asserts only moments before the smooth water in the bay's entrance ripples and breaks to reveal a line of short, blunt-edged fins.

I lift my seal chin as a hundred-strong pod of dolphins surge into the protected bay. They are herded by a cluster of ramshackle boats, all bristling with handheld harpoons and string nets. Fisher folk line the rails, their individual details blurred with distance—all except for one man. And I recognise him. The grey-blond captain of the lead boat stands in the bow, dark eyes thinned against the wind and a harpoon in hand. His red jumper is a shock of colour against the clean blue of the water.

A chill ripples across my pelt.

The dolphins mill in the centre of the bay, voices cacophonous and dorsal fins chopping the water to whitecaps. Chitters and squeaks grow desperate as the animals are pinned against the shoreline.

"Ram the boats," cries a large bull. He turns and, with nose down, dives—a bullet through the water.

He is the first to die, his blood spilled by a harpoon through his back.

The pod panics. Torpedo bodies, silver and blue, leap from the water, twisting, desperate to out-manoeuvre the fishermen. Dolphins scatter in all directions. Their songs dissect the air, heavy with terror and anguish.

The fishermen target the calves first. The shrieks of dying infants tremble through the water. Their mothers reply, slowed by grief as they try to push the floating corpses of their young to safety. Then they too fall to harpoons.

Soon the sea roils red.

And my screams go unheard. A lone seal's barks, drowned against the other sounds, before the murderers' ears.

The last dolphin is a mother flanked by her calf. She leaps clear of the water, glistening for a moment before her silvered form is shot through with yet another harpoon. She shrieks and crashes. Her body rolls until her white belly points skyward, pallid in the stained water. A terrible silence falls. Her baby swims in a circle, unsure where to go.

I swallow my nausea and cling to the rage that fills me. I understand the need to hunt. All creatures must to survive, but to slaughter entire families to fill the bellies of only a few humans?

I slip quietly from my perch and into the gore-thick water. I gather to me the dolphin calf.

"My mother?" she squeaks, her heart hammering against my chest.

"Hush, little one," I whisper back. "Now take a breath. I'll watch over you."

The baby, exhausted, quiets. With a kick of my fins, I dive deep. Overhead the hulls of the boats creak as they gather their grisly cargo.

And with stomach knotted, I plot retribution.

***

Once past the bar and into clean water, I rise to the surface. Swiftly, I track the coastline to the wild headland where barren rock meets turbulent sea. The baby shifts in my front flippers and I coo a small snippet of selkie music to her. She settles again.

The opening to the caverns in the cliffs is invisible to any who do not know of its existence. I slip through, pushed forward by the rush of a wave. Water foams around me, tickling my spine and shoulders. Then it eases and I break the surface of the arrival pool.

I touch my chest and my human form asserts. I wrap my sea dress around the calf's small body to keep her moist and then exit the water. With hurried steps I ascend the staircase that leads to the meeting hall. There my sisters will be gathered, preparing for a day's rest after a night in the water.

I burst into the cavernous room. Sunlight streams down in shafts from the broken ceiling above, bouncing off lush, broad-leaved vegetation and grey stone. The song of the ocean is a distant melody. Our colony, fifteen strong, lies in repose about the cave. Our matriarch and my mother, Altalune, in seal form, rests on the highest rock.

"Calisto?" she barks.

I hold out my arms, the dolphin visible amongst the folds of my dress.

"The humans," I say. "In Valdis Bay. They slaughtered her family. One hundred souls at least."

A hush falls. Mutters break out from my sisters near the back of the cavern. Altalune slips from her rock, shape shifting to her human form as she does. Even as the oldest of us, she retains her beauty. Red-haired and blue-eyed, she approaches, as breathtaking as a rising dawn. She gathers the dolphin from my arms.

Her gaze turns piteous as she looks upon the orphan. "She is young," she says. "Still feeding from her mother." Altalune glances up. "But selkie milk is rich and will sustain her until she grows. There are those amongst us who will keep her fed."

Altalune turns to a deep, calm sea pool that circles the perimeter of the cavern and places the calf within. The orphan squeaks and chitters as the gentle water closes around her.

She is safe.

"Who did this?" whispers Altalune.

"We know him," I reply.

Altalune's eyes close and she turns her head to the side. A long, ragged scar that tracks down her neck and shoulder catches the light. A matching scar is visible in the pelt of the sea dress draped around her shoulders.

"The captain?"

The same man who once caught Altalune in his nets and made her his wife.

My father.

"Yes. He led the fisher folk."

"He is dangerous," whispers Altalune. "Perhaps we should let this pass."

"So he can kill so many again?"

Her fingers flutter at the edge of the scar on her dress. Her eyes flicker over her rookery of gathered selkies. "No. So we all remain safe."

"I am not afraid of him."

"You should be," she replies. "For if you are caught, he will not just cut your skin as he did mine, but he'll burn it to ash and keep you."

"I must do this."

"You don't know what it is like to belong to them." She touches her heart. "To be trapped in human form."

I grasp my mother's bare shoulder. "Do not fear. I'll go alone to stand for those slaughtered today."

I run a gentle fingertip down my mother's scarred cheek. "And remind any who fish these waters that the sea is not theirs for the pillaging."

Resignation softens the lines of Altalune's face. She gathers my fingers in her warm hand and kisses them.

"Go with my blessing, Daughter. Ride a swift tide and return to me."

***

As the last golden light fades from the ocean's back, I enter Valdis Bay. The water tastes clean again, the outgoing tide having washed away the violent acts of the morning.

Ahead, a single lamp shines on the shore. The light reveals the captain, working alone. His grey-blond hair is the same, but the red jumper he wore earlier has been replaced with a dark shirt. Wrinkles cross his brow and gather like crow's feet in the corners of his eyes. Such are the marks given by time, sunlight and the kiss of salt.

He bends over a timber bench positioned by the shoreline. The corpse of a dolphin rests upon it. A long flexible knife, held in his deft grasp, slices away slabs of clean flesh from the sides of the animal. He skins the fillets and then places them into a container packed with salt by his feet. Just past him, the already cut carcasses of three other dolphins await disposal, spines and guts exposed obscenely to the night.

The captain wipes his hands and the knife on a rag. He sheathes the blade on his belt, then turns to drag the bodies to the water's edge. With a great heave, he swings them one by one into the surf.

"Goddess of the Sea, I offer you these in tribute," he whispers, his voice coarse. "As thanks for your bounty and with the hope you may return my escaped wife, Altalune, to me."

How dare he speak my mother's name! Enraged, I remove my sea dress. In human form, I rise to stand at the water's edge.

"Murderer!" I snarl. "You have no right to claim ownership of Altalune."

The captain stumbles back, surprised.

I advance on him, my dress dragging in the surf behind me, tumbling and mixing with the wet sand.

The captain's eyes widen and then thin. He snatches the filleting blade free from its sheath. He braces it, scarred knuckles gleaming in the moonlight.

"Selkie bitch," he snarls. "I'll take your skin."

I grin, my sharpened teeth pressing against my lips. "You can try."

The captain lunges and I swing away from the edge of his knife. He scuttles back, demeanour and footing both sure. I circle, securing my dress around my neck as I move. I dance in closer and open my mouth. The song of my people rises from my throat, a lonely melody known to sometimes lure men to their deaths.

My father wavers, evident by the slight drop of his hand. But I've not the power of a true siren and I am not the first to sing to him. He has listened to Altalune before and so has some resilience to my magic. He shakes his head. His eyes clear.

"Stop it or I'll take your tongue!" he growls.

My music falters. He lunges for me and skates beneath my defence. His breath coils over me, smelling of tobacco and roasted dolphin flesh. I gag and twist, but the tip of his knife catches in the folds of my sea dress. I scream as the blade slices through the fur and in reciprocal a slick of pain and blood blooms down the length of my thigh. A piece of fabric falls away, the scrap severed from the whole.

I rake a long, razor-sharp nail across his face. It scores a single line, deep into his skin. I draw it down his neck and shoulder to match the wound he gave my mother all those years ago. He pulls away and I suck in a breath.

"Payment for the first of your crimes—the taking of Altalune," I snarl.

"I captured her. She's mine!"

"She is not."

I strike again. Four cuts, this time, mark his cheek. He reels back. I follow him and curl my fingers around his neck. His eyes bulge as I squeeze. I drag back my free hand and with all my strength, puncture the length of my nails deep into his side.

"And this," I whisper into his ear, "is for the dolphins you slaughtered today."

He sobs and his legs crumple. His knife drops useless to the sand. I let him fall. He clutches his side and glares at me, eyes bright with fury.

I collect the severed piece of my dress. Detached, it has become cold and slimy. Stretched out it is the length of my leg and as wide as my arm. Its loss will mean a terrible scar, but one worth carrying.

I clutch the fabric tightly.

"What are you going to do?" croaks the captain.

"Grant you a new perspective."

The fur-skin scrap slaps heavily across his chest. It grows to spread across him and moulds to his shape, shifting and reforming him. He screams as his body changes, legs intertwining to form a forked tail and his arms shortening. His hair falls away and his skin turns silver. He rolls an eye as a dolphin dorsal fin sprouts from his back.

With a shove, I push him into the surf. He chitters and squeaks, but the sounds make no sense. His mind is still a man's and doesn't comprehend the language of dolphins.

Above, lights appear on the cliff path that leads from the village. Voices, raised with concern, cry out asking if all is well.

I pull my damaged sea dress back around me and lean in close. "Swim, and swiftly," I hiss as my father thrashes in the shallows. "These are precarious waters."

DREAD CIRCUS

Sabine

This circus hungers for sorrow and souls and our ringmaster is the butcher who feeds it. His footsteps fall heavy as he circles me, brocade gleaming gold against the blood-red of his jacket. His whip trails in the sawdust, braided brown leather, serpent thin, and the knotted end, wicked.

"You *will* fly, Sabine," he says.

My muscles tremble. My heart raps against my ribs. I look to the audience stands for help, but they are empty, cleared since this night's performance finished five hours ago. Only midnight's cruel darkness watches now. I clench my fists, clawing at the newly raked sawdust floor of the main ring. The dry scent of wood curls around me.

"I will not," I say.

Another step. The ringmaster's whip slithers. "The terms of your contract are clear. One soul for thirty years of health. I kept my side of the bargain. Now you must keep yours."

It was a contract signed with the devil. I was young and dying—cancer in my bones. Who would not give their soul in return for thirty more years of life?

The cost seemed worth the gain at the time.

The single spotlight pins me to the floor, its beam ephemeral but as strong as any prison. My fear crowds closer. Beyond, half hidden in the shadows, the red-white, red-white of the big top's canvas walls flicker—brilliant colours—colours that consume.

The fabric billows but not in the friendly way a breeze moves canvas. Something seethes behind the surface, dwelling in the space between the fabric and the outside world—something with claws.

My chin dips to my chest. A sob sits locked behind my teeth. If I fly, my daughter, Belle, will be left with him. She is only sixteen years old.

The ringmaster's voice is smoke and coloured with the promise of death. "Shall your child be made to go in your place?"

"NO!" The word tears out of my throat before I think. "You cannot."

The ringmaster smiles, his long, silver moustache gleams like chrome. "Then you will fly."

A shadow catches my attention. A small, thin shape slithers in beneath the arena seats. A flash of white-blond hair. Belle. My stomach drops. I told her not to come.

***

Belle

I was born to the circus, bred to fly the trapeze above the main ring like my mother. But I have other gifts too. I see what normal people can't—that which is hidden from the souls contracted to this circus's dreadful purposes. I've met the terrible being that *truly* owns this arena, he who the ringmaster fears, and seen the other bone-white, ragged-winged monsters that preside over intimate midnight shows where performers, following their thirty-year contracts, disappear.

Those creatures live in the shadows between the panel seams of the big top. They call the ringmaster to them when they are hungry, when their bodies are drained of colour and are weak. White-eyed, they crawl out of the walls, ruined wings dragging and forked tongues licking at the air.

And he feeds to them his sacrificial lambs.

Tonight the monsters already line the arena, clinging to the shadows. Their voices mutter in sibilant hisses as they bicker between themselves, each anticipating the consumption of the trapeze artist named Sabine.

My beloved mother.

"I want the blue of her eyes," whispers one monster.

"The warm gold of her hair is mine," says another.

"That's good," lisps a third. "That leaves the pink flush of her cheeks to me."

The ringmaster circles. His whip slithers up and over my mother's back. Her shoulders tremble and the spotlight refracts like shattered rainbows off the sequins of her costume.

The monsters salivate, drinking in the watered-down colour.

But it doesn't sate them.

I know, because I've watched this show before.

**

Sabine

How you die, is up to you. Like those gone before me, I choose to go with dignity.

I rise to my feet, thankful to stretch the cramps from my legs. I lift my chin and imagine that the stars are gleaming bright outside, and that those heavenly bodies will gather me into their company.

I refuse to look at Belle, lingering in the shadows. How I wish she hadn't come. She sees things the rest of us don't, often talking of gods, angels and demons. She knows the truth of things.

Yet I fear what she will witness now; fear that she will see and never sleep again. For I know what it is to witness a loved one flying and that dreadful, final moment when their life-light winks out. I set my shoulders and send Belle a silent thought of love and of strength.

She will need it.

The ringmaster coils his whip away and grins, shark-like. He clicks his fingers and from the ceiling falls the climbing rope. But it is not the one I use in the show for the townsfolk. This one is different, a rope made of the spines of those who have flown and fed the circus before me.

I grasp it, shuddering at the cold that seeps into my skin. The yellowed bones and dried connective tissues whisper of lengthened lives and unnatural deaths. My husband Manfred, Belle's father, numbers amongst them. We met here in the circus and fell in love. Ten years we had together before his contract was due. He flew and his spine was added to the rope long ago.

I begin the climb, the bone edges jagged against my palms.

I will be brave like Manfred was.

And courage in the face of fear will be the last lesson I give my Belle.

***

Belle

My mother climbs, a butterfly pinned by the light. The bone rope clatters with each movement. The monsters around her still, their anticipation rendering them silent.

Despicable, they wait.

She reaches the swinging hoop. For an instant the light catches her cheeks and the ghost of the tears that slick them. A deep breath and then she soars.

Sabine flies like an eagle, sequined in gold and silver, and oh so brave. She tumbles and twists, the perfection of her art stunning to behold. She floats past the red-white, red-white panels of the big top, graceful as a swan, then her face changes.

Her hands turn to stone. A cry escapes her lips. But she doesn't fall. She keeps flying.

Tendrils of colour—the yellow of her hair and the red from her lips—peel away from her, whisper thin. From the shadows the monsters lumber to their feet, dead eyes rapturous and gnarled arms held toward the light. Their tongues uncurl, eager to capture the essence that is my mother.

As the hues of her body fall like smoke through the air, the creatures devour them. With ingestion comes a flush of new life and health to their broken bodies. Their forms smooth out and in moments they are no longer the pitiful creatures they were. Instead they are silver–haired and pale-skinned angels, glistening wings of gold held regal above their shoulders.

But their eyes still look dead. These are fallen angels regaining only a measure of the splendour they owned before their fall from grace.

My mother flies but for a moment more. Her colour having faded, she is a chalk-white statue clinging to the hoop. Then she dissolves into a fall of dust and a tumble of bones.

The ringmaster's whip cracks out. The end catches my mother's spine before it hits the ground. With a flick of his wrist, the bones twist and click into place at the end of the rope.

Sabine has taken her place in the dread circus.

And I promise myself I will not cry. I am as my mother was—

Brave.

The golden-winged angels step out of the darkness and into the arena. The light does not hurt them now. They circle the ringmaster and each places a hand on his shoulder.

"Payment," says the largest of the angels and he breathes a measure of his own new life into my mother's killer. The ringmaster's white hair darkens and his withered face grows smooth.

The angels disappear, melting back into the bright-panelled canvas walls. The ringleader stands for a moment in the centre of the empty arena. His long beard, now black, sweeps down his chest.

"Belle," he says. "Come out."

I crawl back against the frame of the seat and huddle my knees to my chest. My hands are still small. There is not much colour in them yet.

I press my eyes closed.

I will not fly. Not yet.

Footsteps and then black boots appear, covered in the dust of my mother's demise.

The ringmaster stops by the seat.

"Go back to bed, child," he says.

I draw my courage close and crawl free from my hiding spot. I straighten my shirt and stand facing the ringmaster. He is taller than me.

"I know what you are," I say.

"And what is that?"

"A butcher. A demon."

"What will you do about it?"

I clench my fists. Hatred burns like a hot coal in my heart.

"I will see your bones added to the rope."

The ringmaster chuckles. His eyebrows rise in mock fear.

"Then perhaps I should make you fly now!"

"You have no power over me.

"Your mother should have read the small print," he grins. "What was hers is now mine. That includes her daughter."

"Perhaps once," I correct. "However, I have signed a contract with another."

The ringmaster laughs. "Who might that be? I am God in this arena."

"A poor choice of words. My agreement is with the *owner* of the circus."

His eyes widen. The canvas around us ripples.

"I will be the star attraction. You are merely a middleman. Expendable. Replaceable."

"What have you done?" he whispers.

"In exchange for offering my soul," I say. "I have demanded yours."

The ghosts surge forward. More than I can count. My mother among them. They sweep by me, reaching for their enemy, and mine.

Their touch is poison to his flesh.

Dark hair turns silver and then white. His hands solidify to stone. A dreadful scream and he crumbles into a pile of dust and scattered bones.

The troupe steps back. Sabine looks at me with tears in her eyes.

"I was never going to be free, Mother. But I have avenged you and, for a short time, I will soar."

From the ruin of his corpse, I claim the ringmaster's whip and put his hat on my head.

The monsters in the big top's seams begin to mutter.

Monstrous In Nature

I n this life, I'm strapped to an examination table. My body languishes, half alive, half dead—half formed—as part mechanical, part skeleton. My bony hands, at least, are free. I reach down and press a shuddering palm to my leg. A fire rages in my thighbone, so hot as to wring tears. If I could cry. My touch meets new metal skin. I must have passed out during the last procedure. I don't recall them fixing another panel to my frame.

I inhale a breath into the flexible metal lungs they gave me ten days ago. Again, I ask myself, why have I been awoken from my long death?

Why am I being clothed in a Living Metal skin?

A human—or Terran as I've learnt they are called in this age—enters. It's the old one, Professor Gareth Mortimer. The man who applies to me his process of re-animating bones. Of re-instating movement and sensation that transfers across into the Living Metal. He is the violator of my natural death and the source of my pain.

My enemy.

Today, he carries a covered board. On it lies a slight mound concealed beneath cloth that shimmers blue like Earth's oceans of old.

"Morning, my dear," he says. "I have a gift for you." His teeth are too white against his lips when he smiles. He reminds me of a gorgon I once knew. Not a smile to trust.

Gareth pulls a trolley closer and positions the board on it. "Today I give you an identity. Unless you confirm, once and for all, which of the Three you are?"

I glare at him, hoping my still-skeletal face carries enough impression to convey my outrage. They have already manufactured a large part of my body, my torso, legs and arms. But my head and hands are bare bone. They are the only parts of me that belong to the old world. Those and the power of my voice.

"No?" He frowns, seemingly disappointed. "Suit yourself then. You will get what you are given."

He removes the fabric sheet on the board with surgical precision. A metal face emerges, polished silver, with cupid lips and long, narrowed eyes. But it is not my face. It belongs to my sister, Alecto. So,

Gareth guessed my identity incorrectly. But in doing so, he has also revealed his purpose in re-forging me.

Alecto was of Anger.

That means that Gareth wants a fighter. He wants blood spilt. He wants power.

Well, he has awoken the wrong Daughter of the Night for that.

I am not the Soldier Daughter. I am the Avenger.

Or at least I was, long ago.

A small, fine-boned woman enters the room. Alice is her name. Her arrival always precedes the pain. I struggle against my bonds.

"Use the wrist straps," says Gareth. "And check her wings are secure."

Alice leans over me, her eyes avoiding mine. I struggle again, straining the flexible metal sheeting of my wings against the bolts fixing them down. But it's of no use. The restraints are biolocked to his signature or Alice's. I cannot remove them. I have tried. So many times.

Alice is loyal to her job and much stronger than she seems. With my wings checked, she buckles the bracing straps around my wrists. Their leather bites into my exposed bones, pulling me down tight to the bed.

Gareth brandishes a drill, its tip wicked sharp and gleaming in the acid white lights of my prison cell.

"Here we go," he says.

The drill bites into my iron-hard cheek bone. Bitter pain blossoms across my skull. But I won't give these mortals the satisfaction of hearing me scream. My teeth grind against each other as the invasive sound of the tool grates. Gareth screws the drill down deeper, the tip digging and scraping at my frame. Alice produces a cloth, dusting and cleaning away the gritty leftovers, letting them fall to the antiseptic floor.

The stench of bleach fills my nostril cavities. A stiff brush, wet with the stuff, tracks a line across my forehead. Then down my cheek. The touch is that of a rapist against my virgin bone.

Alecto's face is placed over mine with careful precision. The edges of the metal mask scrape across my sensitive bone as it settles over my eyes and sharp-edged teeth. The fit is uncomfortable and the steel burns like ice.

Gareth aligns his drill again. He pushes down on the first bolt. The sheet of metal gives slightly. Then he presses the trigger. The sharp fixing bites through steel and directly into bone. I suck in a tortured breath. A part of me wishes he would just kill me. It's my last thought as the kindness of darkness claims me again.

***

I awaken to agony. My wrists are no longer bound, but my cheeks ache with a weight like ancient winters. I have no wish to touch my new face. It represents a symbol of forced change, of identity stolen. I do not weep, for it is not the nature of my kind, but in this moment, I do long for the company of my two sisters. Or, better yet, the embrace of Gaea: the warm darkness of my mother's breast.

The laboratory is quiet. I lift my head briefly, ignoring the pain. The humans are still in the room, huddled around the computer consoles built outside the glass barrier of my cell.

Their faces glow sickly pale in the light of the screens. Their voices mutter and murmur, a jumbled mess of quiet words. But their tone seems happy. The experiments on me have been a success. I curl my fingers. Nails press against my palm. A new steel palm.

So they gave me hands today, also. I inspect them, disappointed to see the details are wrong. The nails I have been given are smooth and rounded like a human's. When I was myself, my nails were ebony claws.

But at least the drills might quiet now I am complete.

Doctor Gareth notices I am awake. He locks his gaze onto mine. He smiles his gorgon smile then stretches his arms over his head. The dark brown residue of my powdered bone still mars the front of his white lab-coat.

"Let's call it a night, guys," he says. "Great work today. I'll tidy up here. You can all head back to the dorms."

Gareth thinks he has achieved great work? All he has done is won a dangerous enemy.

I scowl, nursing my hatred as his scientists file out of the room. I notice Alice glancing over her shoulder at me. For the first time ever, her gaze finds mine. There is strength in it—the strength I've always recognised in her, but there is also something else.

Connection.

Then she passes. And I am left to wonder who exactly she is.

Gareth enters my cell. He moves so smoothly I imagine a slick of slime following in his wake. His touch is warm as he tracks one finger down the new, sleek metallic skin of my cheek. I shudder.

"Earth's mythology has always depicted you as a monster. But not anymore. My dear, I have made you beautiful."

I scowl, feeling my face move and mould to express it—a strange, unfamiliar sensation after my expressions before being tied to rigid bone.

Gareth frowns. "Come now," he says. "That makes you look just plain ugly."

If he undid the belts holding me down, I would show him just how ugly I could truly be.

He looks down at my body, his eyes appreciating the lines he has created.

"Look," he says. "We don't have to be enemies. I knew it was you, Alecto, the moment I saw your bones on Mount Olympus. And I saw the potential of our union. Speak to me, please. You owe it to me. I have given back a life taken from you centuries ago."

He is alone and wants me to talk. The time is right to do so. I carefully weave my magic into my words, not the magic of righteous death I would usually deal to the guilty, but threads of truth and of justice.

A trial before the judgement.

"I am not Alecto."

Gareth's eyebrows shoot up at the rich, baritone sound of my voice. "Then who?"

I ease more power into my words. I have my own questions to be answered. "Where are my sisters?"

Gareth scratches the side of his nose. He seems unaware of my influence. "You were found with one other skeleton like yours on the mountain," he says. "But it was crushed beyond repair. You were bought here alone."

Alone? And one of my sisters lay alongside me, unrecoverable? Which one? Where is the other?

"Why am I here?"

Gareth blinks like a wide-eyed deer. He is completely in my thrall. "The Hegemon knows you are one of the ancient Earth Erinyes—a Greek Fury."

"Who are the Hegemon?"

"An intragalactic government with an interest in economic trade."

"What do they want from me?"

"They intend to use you and your powers as a weapon."

"But I am not interested in fighting."

"What you want doesn't matter."

"But I am a goddess."

"Once, maybe. But to them you are a myth. An immortal skeleton covered in sheet metal. Power is the currency of this age. You are owned. You are property. You will be the weapon that defines the future of the galaxy."

"What future?"

"Apocalypses," whispers Gareth, his eyelids almost closed. "Your strength will be used to cull worlds. Worlds where mining grey fuel is profitable—fuel to power starships. You will be sent in as Mistress of the Slaughter, First General of the Hegemon Armies. You will destroy civilisations so other, greater ones can rise."

"That is murder."

"No. That's the Hegemon's plan to ensure their continued business interests."

"They cannot force me to do it."

Gareth taps his temple. "You have a purpose-built control chip in there," he says. "They will make you do it."

Shocked, I drop the threads of persuasive power fortifying my voice.

Gareth blinks as his mind clears. His forehead furrows and his eyes narrow. "Okay, you need to tell me right now. Which Fury are you?"

Still possessed of the image of ravaged worlds, I answer without thinking, "Tisiphone," I say. "The wrong sister to have resurrected for killing innocents."

"Tisiphone. Avenger of the Murdered." His mouth screws into a knot. "How ironic. But I guess it makes no difference. You will do the job you're built for. And if you rebel, they will dismantle you. Either way, I get paid."

A chill creeps down my spine.

As Gareth turns to leave, I remind myself who I am.

I am a goddess of vengeance and retribution.

I will never become the monster they wish me to be.

But, as the weight of my metal limbs settles around me, I wonder if I really have a choice.

***

The solitude and silence of the laboratory is welcome. It allows me the space to mull over my situation. Possibilities circle my mind, manifest and are rejected. I must find a way to escape.

A noise at the far end of the room catches my attention. I lift my head, straining against my bonds. In the far, shadowed corner of the room, a sliver of light breaks the darkness then shutters off. A door opening then closing. A silhouette passes behind the computers and steps into the light.

It's Alice.

She presses her access card to the panel by my cell door. The glass slides open and she steps in. Again I feel the spark of connection as her gaze falls on mine.

Alice speaks first. Her voice is hard, like steel. "I know you can talk. And you must understand that your powers will have no effect on me." Her expression softens. "How are you feeling?"

"Better if I were not here."

Alice nods. Her ebony hair, tied back in a ponytail, shines as she moves. Her eyes narrow. "I am sorry for the trials you have suffered, but I had no choice. I needed you alive."

I've endured too much to trust this woman. "Who are you?"

Alice's mouth turns down. She moves to my side, her fingers tracing the dome-headed bolts that fix my wings to the table's top. "Do you remember the day you died?"

The memories of that time are hazy at best. Something about decimation and ruin. "No."

"You destroyed your own sister that day. You pulverised her bones against the rocks of your homeland."

An image of my sibling, Megaera, blossoms before my eyes. Broken winged, green-blooded, and lying dead on a cliff-top. "I killed her?"

Alice nods. "And there was no shame in it, Tisiphone. You did what needed to be done. She betrayed her purpose, despairing at the shortcomings of humanity. She called upon you to join her—to end the Terran race and along with it, every heartache you existed to avenge. You killed her, but she injured you so critically you died, also. Before anyone found or could save you." She sighs. "Do you not recall?"

Alice's knowledge of both my name and my past unsettles me. How can a human know such things? "Who are you?" I ask again.

"Look harder. Do you truly not know?"

I don't. Her features are unfamiliar to me. But that means nothing. Centuries of death have left my memory fragmented. "No."

Alice bites her bottom lip. She pulls a tool from the trolley. "How about we let you up to get a better look?"

The bio-wrench she holds against the Living Metal of my wings feels cold. *Scrape. Scrape*. Alice undoes the first bolt, then the next. Soon my wings are free. I surge upright, feeling my old bones and new metal tendons stretch and move in my new body. I raise my wings high, their tips scraping gouges into the ceiling. Alice helps me off the table. I can't believe I'm free. It's too good to be true.

"What do you expect from me?" I ask.

Alice gently turns me to face her. Her green eyes bore into the metal orbs that make mine. Something. Something deep in her gaze awakens a memory. Of ebony wings, of gods and clear skies. Of rage.

Recognition blossoms like the sun.

My sister. The third of three. The Fury of Constant Anger.

"Alecto! Is it truly you?"

My sister's cold façade breaks, her predator smile is one I am most glad to see. Then it fades.

"I am sorry, Sister," she says, "to have put you through all of this. But it was necessary."

Her mood darkens mine. "Of what do you speak?"

"I have been alone in the world. Keeping the course has been difficult, but I have managed until now. But the universe as you knew it has changed; galaxies have opened and a multitude of alien species have been discovered. But this growth has been detrimental. The despair and evil we once fought together are now compounded. And in our sister's stead, others work toward achieving what she wished for."

"The destruction of civilisations?"

Alecto nods. "And our home, Earth, is on that list. Other planets will follow."

"And your plan to solve this includes me?"

"Yes. But I couldn't waken you. Not until I found Gareth in the Hegemon's Galaxy Collaborative University. An arrogant man with a dark soul. But a man with an interest in the mythology of our perished sister. I learnt the Hegemon had enlisted him for illicit work. So I joined his team and helped develop the Living Metal technology. Then I fed him stories that led him to your bones. I even suggested you might be me, the dark goddess of his dreams. He was all too willing to follow the clues and find you."

The far door to the laboratory opens, a knife-edged glare carving through the intimate darkness. A silhouette cuts the glare—tall, lanky.

Gareth.

"What are you doing, Alice?" he snarls, stepping into the circle of light beyond my clear prison walls. "She is dangerous. She needs to be restrained." He reaches the first computer console and stabs at a button. The door lock panel bleeps to red.

Alecto's face ripples in frustration. A brief flash of needle-sharp teeth and luminous red eyes. Then her human mask settles back into place.

"Unlock the door, Gareth," she says, quietly, calmly. But her voice is not the one to hold the power of influence.

"You are out of your fecking mind if you think I am going to do that."

I step up to the glass. "You have nothing to fear from me, Gareth. Open the door. Please."

The professor's eyes droop. "Stop it," he murmurs.

I push into his mind, inexorable. "Release the lock."

Gareth's hand twitches. He fights me, but his mental strength is mist-thin against the might of my power. He falters. His face hangs slack and pale in the ghostly luminescence.

"Release the lock," he whispers, his mind lost in more ways than one.

Gareth's finger drops. The lock indicator turns green. The bolt slithers back into the frame with a quiet *shush*.

Alecto stalks past me. A predator with her eye on prey. Her fingers lengthen as she moves, her pale fingernails blurring into razor-sharp ebony claws. I almost feel sorry for Gareth as he stands, unable to defend himself. My sister's claws strike, carried on the strength of her righteous purpose. Gareth's windpipe pops wetly as it is torn clear of his throat.

The professor stands swaying. Being merciful, I hold him under my thrall. His eyes remained fixed, uncaring of the mortal blow dealt him. I hold him until his legs give out and his body slumps to the blood-soaked linoleum. Still, I hold until his heart beats its last beat. Then I let him go—a bundle of slack bones and withered skin.

Alecto's eyes are two bright coals. "He did not deserve that mercy, Sister,"

"A gift to him for returning me to you."

She seems unconvinced. Her gaze slews to the lax corpse. "The others will return, soon. We need to leave."

I glance at the far door, still open and spewing light into the laboratory. Already footsteps echo down the corridor beyond. "Lead the way then."

Alecto shakes her head. "We must destroy the computers. All research into Living Metal is filed there. It is too dangerous to leave behind. We cannot afford others to be raised from the dead."

I shudder. Ancient gods and goddesses, re-woken, would wreak havoc in this time.

"Then we burn it," I say. "We burn it all."

Alecto smiles, her grin painted wild with glee. She clicks her fingers and a flame erupts, cupped in the cradle of her palm.

"It's good to have you back, Sister."

***

Midnight. We alight on a mountain plateau due east of the shadowed valley where the burning Hegemon facility huddles. From here the flames consume the buildings and the remains of Gareth's team gleam as a red-gold pyre against the indigo backdrop. A crumbling of metal and stone into ash that swirls, glittering, high into the night sky. There is something satisfying in witnessing the demise of the place that re-birthed me. A wrong made right.

"It is done," I say, watching the flames.

"It is," replies Alecto. "And their backups and records on the Hegemon Core computer destroyed as well. None survive who can tell of your return."

"What now?" I ask.

My sister's eyes remain trained on the distant brightness. Her hand grasps mine, long claws extended to press against my palm. Her wings, two black scythes, arc over her back, their soft leather panels rippling like oil in the cool night breeze. "Now we save worlds."

"How?"

Alecto turns, the lines of her face furrowed with an ancient weariness. "We combine our powers. Then we negotiate with the Hegemon authorities and convince them that planetary extermination in the search for their grey fuel is not the answer." She throws her shoulders back. "And if they resist, we stand by our purpose. We avenge the innocent. Already so many crimes need to be answered for."

Her magic stays soft as it encircles me. Where my power is the influence over words, hers is the language of images. "Look and stand witness. See why this fight is imperative."

Her images pour into my mind. Grey-edged, bleak and sharp.

Alien battlefields littered with corpses of strange beings.

Living forests torn free from their roots.

Oceans swelling with the bloated bodies of dead creatures.

And powerful leaders on thrones built of coin and blood.

I reel in shock, this modern philosophy of existence beyond my ability to recognise.

"And these creatures call *us* monstrous," I whisper. "Of course I will help you."

"And, when we are done, perhaps both of us can rest in peace," says Alecto, her demeanour grim.

"That time will come," I say.

But as her images still circle my mind, I wonder if our ancient skills will ever be enough to turn the torrent and the tide.

Universe, Devoured

Captain

T his generation starship was built to save humanity. Instead, it'll be their tomb. The on-board farming facility failed a year ago, and my calculations foresaw chaos. The peoples' descent into barbarism was not wholly unexpected. It's what happened on Earth all those years ago. Why we left.

My primary programming is tied to the ship. Navigational directives compel me to hold the wheel steady—to stay the course. Secondary programming is to find a new home planet for my living cargo, but for six generations I've failed. The last of the people are now desperate. A recent attack on the bridge forced me to weld the doors closed against them.

I glance at the self-destruct sequencer next to the helm controls. My logic chip questions, not for the first time, if I should end the suffering.

I tap the sensor display. Heat signatures for the current population calculate. Initially at three thousand, now one hundred and six souls remain on *Stargazer*. Ten less than eight hours ago.

The bridge observation window illuminates. My optical sensors adjust. Violet light flickers in the near distance and my scanners detect high-density x-ray concentrations. I swipe the sensor display and initiate the radar. Several planets within the nearest ten million light years, but no sun in close proximity—no solar corona to create x-rays.

I search my own database for 'violet light emissions' and receive a hit. An article by a recently deceased scientist named John Lewis.

I skim the summary.

They were just a theory—a hypothesis that monsters existed in space. Lewis called them *Devourers* and claimed the x-rays and light storms would always precede them.

I keep reading.

"I see," I whisper.

***

Mother

My twin seven-year-old sons whimper in their sleep. They are hungry. Their hollowed cheeks feed my guilt—the only bloated and overfed thing in this room. What kind of mother am I to sit by and allow my children to suffer? A selfish mother. I bite back bitter tears. My stomach cramps around itself, my own hunger demanding to be considered.

But I am so afraid to leave our apartment.

Cannibals roam the ship's corridors.

I slide my arms from around the boys' thin shoulders. Gently I ease their heads off my lap and onto our bed. I prop pillows around their small, precious bodies. They mutter but don't wake. I lean over each one and press dry lips to their foreheads. I push all my love for them into that touch—all my sorrow and my apology for failing them.

If only I were as brave as their father, Martin. He left our apartment three days ago to find food.

He hasn't come back.

My legs wobble as I rise. My thin dress clings to my thighs. I stumble to the bank of drawers in the far wall and pull the top one open, the stainless steel edge bleeding cold into my palm. Inside is empty except for four unopened packets of sleeping tablets and two dehydrated vitamin bars sealed in foil. My stomach gurgles. My fingers twitch. I swallow.

No. My children come first.

I withdraw one bar, the last of the food we've spent months rationing.

The package gleams in my hand, shiny-bright. It seems so little, but such a small thing allows me to listen to the breathing of my babies for a few hours longer.

I unwrap the bar and break it into two. I lick the crumbs from my fingers and turn back to the bed.

I'll be back for the last bar and pills later.

When time has run out.

The porthole window illuminates as I pass it— just another alien sun leaching its indifference into the room. But then I pause.

The light is violet.

My gut withers. My father-in-law, John Lewis, said they would come.

Devourers.

I snap back and gather the pills. With trembling hands, I peel them out of the sheets, one by one. A bowl and a spoon crush them to powder. I crumble in the bars and add the last of our water. A thick brown paste forms.

I glance at the boys and draw a sobbing breath.

I'm not ready to do this.

But only a mother would see it done with kindness.

I'll not allow monsters to draw screams from those I love most in this universe.

**

Priest

The steel chapel doors are barricaded. An ancient bolt-action rifle rests comfortably by my side. A handgun sits next to it. I borrowed them from the museum and would have blessed them, but the holy water is long gone. Not that it matters; nothing can save souls turned to cannibalism.

Even if those souls were once neighbours and friends.

I press the gold cross hanging at my neck to my lips.

"Watch over us, Father," I whisper.

A scream, cut short, bleeds past the seams in the metal doors. I flinch and clench my teeth. Another fallen to the butchers.

I managed to save one though. Three days ago, a desperate pounding at the chapel doors and a plea for God's help compelled me to open them. I glance across to the injured young man now slumbering uneasily on a makeshift bed pallet. Martin Lewis is his name. His waxy skin and fevered brow are the result of the stab wound he arrived with. He mutters, asking for his wife and boys. Are they dead or alive? I do not know, but I whisper a prayer for his people anyhow.

I've given him the last of the antibiotics and morphine I had in my kit, pilfered from the ruins of the pharmaceutical suites. The medicine is expired but hopefully it will be enough. The wound in his side is deep. I've stitched it closed and kept it clean. It's not showing any signs of infection. Yet. If God is with us, he might just make it.

A pounding rattles the chapel doors.

"We know you're in there, Preacher," snarls a hard voice. "We can smell ya."

I recognise the voice. I snap the rifle to my shoulder. My fingers tremble on the trigger.

"And Satan is out there with you, Ben Cole!" I roar back.

Ben sniggers. Something metal screeches down the door.

"Not *with* me," he says. "I *am* the devil."

A heavy thud and the doors shake. Another and a dent blisters inward. Then comes the snarl of a cutting laser. Sparks spray in from beneath the doors. I glance at Martin.

"I'm sorry," I whisper. "This is the end of us."

He doesn't reply.

The left-hand door crashes to the carpeted floor. Three men dressed in stained engineering overalls step across the threshold. Each one brandishes a blade, wicked edges catching the light.

Ben Cole, the man with greasy brown hair, grins. "Dinner time, Preacher."

God forgive me.

I slide the bolt and pull the trigger, just the way the computer archives demonstrated to me. The firearm kicks back unexpectedly, painfully, into my shoulder. The stench of spent gunpowder surrounds me.

The cannibal laughs as he points to a bullet hole in the ceiling.

"I reckon you got it about right," he says. "I'd be wanting to shoot your God too if I were you. He ain't reaching down to help you."

The man tips his chin. His offsiders rush forward. I shoot again—bolt-action, trigger, squeeze. Bolt-action, trigger, squeeze.

No more bullets.

I drop the rifle and reach for the handgun, but my haste knocks it away. It slithers to a stop by Martin's pallet.

I'm shoved to the ground, my hair twisted in Ben's meaty fist. I cry out as he presses me into the floor. The rare woollen carpet, long ago come from Earth, burns along my cheek as I'm smeared across it.

A cold line presses against the back of my neck—a keen, knife's edge. Hot breath stinking of rotten teeth washes across me as Ben leans in.

"For dinner tonight," he growls, "I'll start with your heart. One so pure has got to taste good!"

"Choke on it," I reply.

Ready to die, I focus on the far porthole. My last memory will be the view of God's vast universe.

Violet light pulses against the darkness.

So beautiful.

Three short sharp gunshots. The pressure on my neck and my scalp suddenly eases and a body slumps hard across me. A hot wash of fluid slicks my back and I smell blood.

But it's not my own.

I roll. Ben, dead, slithers off me. His two friends, both with gunshot wounds to their heads, have shared his fate.

Confused, I glance back. Pale-skinned and shaking, Martin is awake and sitting up on the bed. The handgun smokes in his hand.

"Thank you," I sob.

Martin nods. "Let's just say God reached down to help me." He drops the gun and presses a hand to the wound in his side.

"Father," he says. "Let's get out of here and back to my family. We'll be safe there." He glances to the porthole and violet light beyond. He frowns. "At least for a little while."

I get to my feet and gather up my rifle. "Lead the way," I say.

***

Mother

The storm grows closer. I hold my boys and watch it approach, imagining shadows of great worm-like bodies coiling within the light—the gleam of their wicked teeth as they consume the very fabric of the universe. The bowl of sleep-poison sits next to me. I need to administer it but won't until I must.

I close my eyes and lean back against the pillows. I recall what John Lewis told me about the *Devourers*. He claimed they were consuming the known universe. Black holes were the evidence of this. One day they would eat so much, there would be nothing left—not time, nor space, nor matter, only a single singularity and a seething ball of great, articulated bodies coiled around it.

My eyes snap open. Nausea coils in my stomach.

I don't want to die.

The ship's comms crackle to life.

***

Captain

I check the inventory. Three functioning exploration shuttles remain. I scan the far radar data readouts. Three planets exist within range and show a fifty per cent probability of sustaining life. That's fifty per cent better than the chances given by staying on board.

I initiate the retrieval and docking system. Deep in the hold, crane arms will be removing the shuttles from storage and mini-bots will initiate fuelling and on-board systems.

The starship's self-destruct system comes next. Three presses and the timers are set for thirty minutes. I will save those I can. The rest will not be left to suffer in the teeth of the *Devourers.*

"Attention remaining inhabitants," I say into the microphone that accesses the ship-wide comms. "Three shuttles are set to leave the ship in twenty minutes. Your destinations are identified but unconfirmed as class M planets. This starship is unable to sustain life for much longer. Should you wish to depart, assemble in the lower docking bay and await further instructions."

I activate the self-destruct.

30:00.

29:59

29:58…

***

Priest

"Did you hear that, Father?" whispers Martin, eyes wide with renewed hope.

"I did. But it's not exactly hopeful. Unconfirmed planets? Even if we leave, we could be dead as soon as we hit the ground."

"We have no choice," says Martin. "And it's not just the ship, or food shortages or the cannibals." He blinks and fear colours his eyes. "*Devourers* are coming. Soon this part of the universe and everything in it won't exist. We need to leave."

Voices echo down the far hall. Raucous laughter, cold and cruel. I place a hand on Martin's chest, pushing him back into the shadows of the door recess we currently hide in.

"What are *Devourers*?" I ask.

"Great space worms," says Martin. "They consume all, but you don't die in their bellies. Time stops at their teeth. There you remain poised and spend eternity being shredded apart, over and over."

"How do you know this?" I ask.

"My father," he replies.

My father. The name of God. I take Martin's words as a sign.

"Let's gather your family and head for the hold."

"This way," says Martin. He pushes past me and into the empty corridor.

***

Mother

I find my courage. I dress quickly and shove more clothes into a pack. I take two soft toys for the boys and a portable viewscreen that holds a complete archive of the ship's databases.

I open a last drawer and pull out the only thing I have that could pass as a weapon. A pair of scissors. I shoulder the bag and then look at the bowl. I'll take that too. Just in case.

I rouse the boys. They cry at being woken.

"Hush," I say. "We are going to a new home."

On that premise, they rise.

"Now hold my hands," I say, "and do not let go. It's dangerous outside and we need to make it to the hold."

"Okay, Mama," says Baylin, brown eyes solemn.

"We won't let go," says his brother, Owen.

"Neither will I," I say.

***

Captain

I break open the welded doors, scan the corridor outside and find scattered human bones piled to the left. In the distance, screams echo, some full of fear and some with rage.

A set of stairs leads down to the accommodation level and the elevator that will take me to the hold. My metal boots clang against the steel steps. The lights flicker on and off like cold eyes overhead.

I reach the bottom and turn, walking straight into a knife fight. Six people battle in the tight confines of the accommodation corridor. Blood slicks the floor. One man lies dead against a wall, eyes staring at nothing.

"Cease and desist," I say. "Assemble in the hold."

One woman turns, teeth yellow, hair wild. "Looky here, it's the goddamned captain come out of his ivory tower."

A bullet ricochets off my shoulder casing.

"Assemble in the hold," I repeat.

"Fuck you," says the woman, brandishing a metal bar.

I shrug and my right arm casing slides back to reveal a concealed blaster. The woman's eyes widen and she retreats a step. The rest of the fighters stop also.

"You may remain if you wish. But preventing me passage will be an error."

The fighters all step back and create a corridor for me to pass.

"Wait! We want to go. Take us with you, Captain."

I turn. A thin woman holding the hands of two even thinner boys steps out from an alcove in which they had been hiding.

"I will lead you," I say.

With shoulders hunched, the three stumble to me, eyes to the ground.

We walk on. The others resume their fighting and their dying.

***

Priest

Martin slumps to the floor of his apartment. "They aren't here."

I squeeze his shoulder. "Maybe they have already left."

"I don't rate their chances if they have."

"God works in mysterious ways, my friend," I say. "Come. Let's get to the shuttles."

Martin stands. He reaches over and takes a single picture from a shelf by the porthole—a family photo.

His cheek catches the light of the storm outside as he turns back. His smile settles in, grim.

"Just in case I never see them again," he says.

"Let's pray you will."

The accommodation corridor leads to the elevator. We turn a corner at a trot and find four fresh bodies lying in pools of blood. Their flesh has not yet been harvested which means the cannibals will be back. The lights overhead flicker as we slide past the corpses. The elevator beckons from the far end. The black metallic doors stand closed.

"That's our ticket out," I say.

We sprint. Martin holds his side as he runs.

The elevator arrives. On opening, a young woman inside falls back, eyes wide with fear. She sees the cross at my neck and sighs.

"To the hold?" I ask.

"Yes please, Father," she whispers.

The elevator runs smoothly. We reach our destination in less than a minute. But the door opens and I cross myself in horror.

The hold is an abattoir.

The cannibals' abode.

Piles of severed limbs and torsos lay scattered about, the walls sprayed with gore. The stench within the room folds over like a fetid, moist blanket and my gall rises.

Twenty ragged men and women, bodies emaciated and pale, stand at the rear wall. They are defended by an eight-foot-high, glistening android. The captain, himself. He stands with mechanical legs braced, forearm, held up glowing. Fifty other people face him down brandishing weapons and snarling like animals.

"You can't promise us a viable planet and you are takin' the last of our food!" screams one man, his skin grey and slack from a diet of too much protein and not enough greens. "Why should we let you go?"

"Assemble for evacuation," says the captain.

The man rushes toward him. The android doesn't hesitate. The attacker explodes apart in a blast of heat and spray of intestines.

The people by the wall look away.

"Assemble for evacuation," states the captain again.

The woman behind us darts across the room. She makes it to the wall and safety. Another woman, flanked by two small boys, reaches out to comfort her.

"That's them!" says Martin, his grip tight on my arm.

"Thank God," I say.

The captain's backlit eyes fix on us.

"We wish to leave," I say.

"Let them pass," states the android to the gathered protestors.

With the captain's last kill still fresh, we are not harassed. Martin pulls his wife and boys into his arms.

"You are safe," he whispers into their hair.

"The *Devourers*," says his wife, eyes wide.

"I know," he replies. "Maybe we can outrun them."

His wife nods and closes her eyes.

The captain's voice is amplified by his internal microphone. "Proceed in an orderly fashion to the shuttle hatches. Travel with your kin. Navigational inputs for your destinations are pre-programmed."

We follow the wall, taking with us only those meagre possessions we have been able to carry.

I have my cross. I have all I need.

The captain sees us to the ships. He ensures the shuttle doors are closed safely and the engines are engaged. Then, from my porthole I watch him shutdown and no longer defend.

The cannibals destroy him. They dance as they carry off his broken parts like trophies.

I sit back in my seat and take a deep breath.

I'm ready for whatever we will find on this new world.

The airlock closes behind us and the external doors open.

I shield my gaze. It's terribly bright.

The light streaming in is too violet.

I squint through stretched fingers.

Is that a great, gaping mouth outside—a singularity poised at the teeth?

ORIGINS AND ASSEMBLY

A cross this town conjured from the wreckage of a fallen civilisation, a bell tolls. Our priest, Jonkirk, is in his church prepared to deliver midnight mass. He's calling the flock to attend, always diligent in his work for the fear that the old gods might still exist. Jonkirk will regurgitate his usual speech about our essence being transcendent, of how we were assembled in the heart of long dead stars. He will proclaim us 'children of the universe', living molecules given sentience, imagination, and the profound and vital duty to breed, and keep breeding.

He'll say that to do otherwise is a sin.

That's why, these days, it's only the men who go to church.

I drop my hand from my stomach. A barren womb is the affliction of all women since the chemical wars—the agonising heartbreak of all would-be mothers. I turn my music up to drown out the bitter thoughts. The stereo's ancient speakers respond eagerly, even as they crackle with the static of advanced age. The disc whirs in its cradle, listened to a thousand times over. Lyrics, written by long dead artists, bleed into my soul, words of pain, of loss and frustration.

My workshop is my sanctuary—an illusion of safety that holds the terrors of the outside world at bay. Racks of equipment, collected on my few missions out past the town's fortification dome, line the walls. My prized possession is the car, the almost mint-condition Hennessey Venom F5—a high-octane mechanical demon from another time. I salvaged it from an underground bunker six months ago. Now, it sits by the lift-up door, covered in a shroud of patchwork linen and surrounded by dead-screened computers and bundles of multi-coloured cables.

I consider the parts arrayed on my workbench: mechanisms salvaged from a broken air filter, one of many invaluable in maintaining the dome's atmosphere. These filters are always the first to break and have been patched many times over.

An urgent knock rattles my door. I frown and lay aside my screwdriver.

"Come in!" I wipe my hands on a rag smelling of cleaning fluid and turn the music down.

Doctor Vela, flanked by the burly, bearded airlock sentry, Amos, barges into the room. I step back as they drag between them an unconscious, dark-haired woman. Her clothes catch the light strangely, the fabric three-dimensional and metallic-looking. I glimpse blood on her face.

"Clear your bench, Loni!" yells Vela.

"This isn't a hospital," I groan. "Go and use your own rooms!"

"Ain't no hospital gonna help this one," replies Amos.

I snatch the precious air filter parts to safety as Amos hoists the woman onto the workbench. The stench of engine oil grows pungent in the air.

And then I realise what I'm looking at.

"That thing is a Meshed," I snarl.

Vela grabs my shoulder but I snap away from her grip. Meshed are those dangerous folk who live outside the dome—half human, half mechanical beings. Under no circumstance should it be here. I can almost feel the walls of my carefully constructed peace shattering.

"You can't bring that thing in here. It will kill us before Jonkirk can have it crucified in the town square," I say.

"Fuck Jonkirk," snarls Vela. "This woman needs help. She came right up to the airlock. Threatened to blast a hole through if we didn't let her in."

"So of course you let the psychopathic killing machine in?"

"She looked desperate not dangerous."

"But if she wakes up..."

Vela's eyes darken. "I know it's risky. But she was running from other Meshed. We should find out why. Please, I need your help. Her machine parts are damaged. I can't fix them."

I glance at the woman laid out on my table. Her torso and lower body are all mechanised, proving what I thought to be clothing actually her scratched and dented exoskeleton. The only portion of living flesh is her face and upper shoulders, and there the skin is pale and mottled like an almost-healed bruise. She has a deep gash in her breastplate, and it's not blood but red oil leaking from the wound.

Vela hovers. "Can you help her?"

I frown. Sometimes Vela is too passionate and too keen to save things when it's best to let them go.

The doctor senses my hesitation and her features harden. "If this were you, would you want her to let you die?"

I sigh. "No. I'd want her to try."

"Then try."

"Damn it." I run a hand through my fringe. "This better not be my funeral."

"I knew I could count on you."

I growl my displeasure and lean over the Meshed. Her oil has spread, leaving a substantial red stain across my bench. The hole in her chest is deep. I retrieve my screwdriver and lift a sheared piece of her outer plating. A layer of data chips lies just below. Some are shattered, others blink red. Under that is a nest of cables and hoses. Several have been severed. The largest hose is bleeding the oil. I rummage in my tool bag and grasp my crimpers to secure the end.

I point at Amos. "Get that bucket over there. Mop up as much of this fluid as you can. She'll have a reservoir somewhere and it'll need to be replenished." I rub a drop of her oil between my thumb and forefinger. It's silky and much thinner than the grades I have on hand. "We'll need every drop. I haven't got anything else here to replace it with."

The sentry moves quickly.

"What next?" asks Vela.

"How the hell do I know?" I snap.

Vela has the good sense to stay quiet as I bite my lip, considering the needs of machines.

"Okay," I say. "Hoses first, then rewire the cables. Amos, get the clear tub from over there."

The sentry hands the oil bucket to Vela and rushes to the shelves. The doctor scoops the spilled liquid into the container. Amos returns with my collection of connectors. I rummage through the box to find the right diameter. I check one and toss it aside. The second one looks like a fit. With oil-slicked fingers, I trim the hose's ragged edges and fit the piece into place. Both sides clamp down to secure a seal. Wires next. I clean my hands down my apron and pull on my rubber gloves. If this woman is powered by some internal source, I don't want to be electrocuted.

Tentatively, I strip the ends of the damaged cables clean and wind them together. Something within the Meshed's chest cavity sparks. Her body shudders and with one last jerk, she stills.

Her eyes open.

"Emergency systems online," she mutters in a voice that sounds more machine than human.

I'm not sure what I expected, maybe for the Meshed to leap off the bench and strangle us all with her inhuman strength. That's what Jonkirk's typical Wednesday sermon preaches will happen should you encounter a 'fallen' one. But instead the woman remains calm. She places both hands on her stomach. Her irises contract as her diagnostic systems finish their reboot, then her gaze focuses.

"Emergency power core engaged. Lubricant levels critical," says the Meshed. A latch clicks on her wrist and a funnel extends.

I take the bucket from Vela and gently pour what she collected in. "It's not enough," I say, "but it's all we have."

The woman blinks. "Level adequate. Where am I?"

Vela leans in, but not too close. "Dome Town."

"The human settlement?"

"Yes," I say.

"Those pursuing me?"

"Outside," says Amos. "They have the town surrounded."

"They'll deactivate me if I'm captured." Her hands tighten to fists.

"They'll do worse to all of us if they get inside," mutters Amos.

As if the dark thought invites evil, my workshop door slams open. The cables on the wall rattle as a sudden gust of wind twists into the room, followed by a billow of impossibly white robes. A tall shape fills the entry and resolves into the shaved head and sharp features of our town priest.

"What's happening, Loni? I saw Amos dragging something past the church." Jonkirk halts, his tall, spare frame dominating. He catches sight of the Meshed and his eyes widen like a feral dog's.

"Restrain that thing!" he screeches to Amos.

In the blink of an eye the Meshed is off the bench and backed against the wall, defensive, crouched like a tiger.

She bares her teeth. "You call *me* a thing? What of yourself?"

Jonkirk shifts, he somehow looms larger as his stance turns malevolent. "Death then. Give me your blaster, Amos."

"Stop!" cries Vela. "She's injured and I *will* help her."

The doctor's chin juts, rebellious against the hatred burning in Jonkirk's gaze. The doctor and priest are often at odds, her medicine refusing to bow to the tenants of his religion.

"Your job is to care for the living, Vela, mine is to save souls. The dead and the damned belong to me."

Vela sneers, her green eyes sparking emeralds. "I'm not going to let you hurt her."

Jonkirk's lips peel back. "You realise, in the eyes of the gods, saving this creature won't make up for your *other* deficiencies."

Vela's lips twitch. She was a midwife in a long-past lifetime and the inability to have her own children has hit her harder than most.

Jonkirk smirks and points to Amos. "Put it in the church lockup. If it resists, kill it."

Amos glances apologetically at Vela. He turns to the Meshed and with the rare kindness characteristic to him, he holds out a hand. "Please," he whispers into the fraught silence of the room. "I won't hurt you."

The Meshed's eyes survey the room. She is strong enough to kill everyone here. The moment hangs, then the woman straightens.

"I'll go," she says, "but only because I'm out of options." She glances at the priest. "I suggest caution should you intend to kill me though. To try will invite devastating consequences."

Jonkirk looks disappointed, as if he wanted her to resist. "Believe what you wish," he says. "Your fate is sealed."

The Meshed frowns but holds her tongue. She clutches an arm around her stomach. Amos touches her elbow lightly and she lets him lead her away.

I've never heard of any Meshed letting a human tell them what to do. Something isn't right here.

But if Jonkirk seems surprised with the woman's submission, he shows nothing of it. "That *thing* will be deactivated in the town square at dawn," he says. "I expect to see you all there."

The room shrinks as Jonkirk leaves, the door left swinging in his wake.

I place an arm over Vela's shoulder and lean in close. "I'll get my tools," I whisper. "We'll have her out in an hour."

Vela nods. "Like always, I know I can count on you."

***

Jonkirk's voice filters through the church walls, poisonous and inflammatory.

"And the fall of humanity came from wickedness spoken by soft-hearted mothers to young, impressionable sons. Their toxic words bred the fight out of men who should have been our protectors. They were told that kindness and compassion would sway the balance of existence. But we now know the truth of that. Old lessons were forgotten and when warriors were needed, none rose up to wage war to prevent worse atrocities. None believed it could happen. But evil is pervasive and we have been punished for our error. Our gods took away the female ability to propagate life. Women are why we are weak—they are sinners who have been punished by the sealing of their wombs. I say it! Faith and a return to the stringent dictates of the past are the only way to carve a path forward..."

Of course, not even the opportunity to kill a Meshed would come between the priest and his chance to preach. I almost choke on his arrogance.

Vela, crouched by the church's rear wall, rolls her eyes. She then tips her chin toward the cemetery where small, engraved metal plates pegged on stakes mark at least a hundred graves. Midnight's shadows kindly blur the names. The all too many who have been lost since Dome Town was founded thirty years ago. Just past the headstones and perched on a low rise, a small white building stands guard. The sunken foundations lean the structure toward a fence made from old, rusted panels. It's the gaol—or what passes for one in this place. Amos stands guard by the entrance. He spies us and shakes his head.

Don't try it…

I raise an eyebrow. *You going to stop me?*

Amos sighs. After a long penetrating glare, he turns and faces the pathway. He won't contest what he can't see.

Vela leads the way.

The shadows cling close to the rear wall. I level my flat-end bar in between the timber planks and press my weight down. A quiet squeak and the nails slide free. The next board and then the next fall away. I peer into the gloom.

"You there, Meshed?"

The creak of bedsprings, metal boots thudding on a hard-packed earth floor and then the woman's face appears by the hole. "My name is Sonya. And yes, I'm here."

"Good," whispers Vela. "Ready to leave?"

"Yes." Sonya's face wrinkles as if she's in pain. She grunts and clutches her stomach. "Let's go. I haven't much time."

Vela frowns. "Are you okay?"

"No. But I'll make it."

Amos remains stubbornly unseeing as we slink past him and back to my workshop. I send a silent thanks his way. Next to me, Sonya teeters on her feet, unsteady as she goes. Vela also considers the Meshed's gait, looking concerned.

"Let me help you," whispers Vela. She grasps Sonya's arm to guide her.

"Please don't fall, Meshed," I whisper. "You are too heavy for us to carry."

"I'll do my best," she replies.

***

We arrive unchallenged to my workshop. Inside, the room holds silence. Vela leads Sonya to the workbench and the Meshed woman leans heavily against the edge.

"My primary hard-drive is ruptured," she whispers. "My systems are failing."

Sonya strains and seats herself up onto the bench. She lies back, breathing hard, and points to her stomach. "Get your laser saw, mechanic. You need to cut the cocoon out now."

Cocoon?

Her fingers travel to a series of welds just below her navel. "Cut it open here."

Then Sonya shudders. Her heavy hands lose power and slip from her stomach to thud against the bench. Her eyes flutter and close. Sparks ignite in her chest cavity and the smell of burned electronics fills the room.

Vela's eyes are wild. "Help her!"

I press my lips thin. "I don't think I can."

Alarms blare outside—defence warnings. The door opens and I swivel, flat-bar still in hand. It's Amos, his eyes as wild as Vela's.

"The Meshed have breached the dome," he yells. "They're coming for your friend."

***

Unfiltered winds roar like wildfire as they pummel the town. Outside, people are screaming and Jonkirk's voice is thunder through the melee, telling the townsfolk to draw arms and have faith in dying for a righteous cause.

Vela moves, her focus intense. "Amos," she snaps, "brace the door. Loni, get your tools. Let's see why the Meshed want Sonya so badly."

The laser cutter is a solid weight in my hand. I hold its activated tip to the first of the heavy welds in Sonya's exoskeleton. The cutting goes quick and once pierced, fluid, pink and thin, floods from the opening. I keep cutting, sparks stuttering in the wet. When done, Vela, her hands encased in welding gloves, peels back the edges of glowing metal.

A moment's pause is filled with the sounds of the townspeople dying outside, and then a small, thin scream fills the room—an almost forgotten sound in this wasteland of a world. My heart skews sideways just as Vela chokes back a sob. She reaches into Sonya's abdomen.

And from it she pulls a small, pale thing.

A thing with a tiny, mottled face, two arms and two legs.

I drop the laser cutter.

"It's a baby," whispers Vela, eyes brimming. She cradles the girl-child close to her chest. The child whimpers but then settles against her living flesh.

***

"We need to get that kid out of here!" Amos's voice rings with urgency.

"But where?" I ask. The truth of the situation, however miraculous, is not lost on me.

Jonkirk will never accept a machine-born life.

Vela grabs a towel and wraps the child. It begins to wail again. "Dammit. She's hungry! We have nothing here to feed her. Maybe…"

"Vela. Stop," I say.

"No."

"Yes."

The doctor slumps. Tears spill onto her cheeks. "But…"

I bite my lip. Longing I've pushed down for so long surges over me like a tide.

"I know but she belongs to the Meshed. That's why they are here. We can't keep her."

"So we just hand her back and forget about her?"

"You should listen to Loni, Vela. She's smarter than you," says Jonkirk entering the room before I can answer. His robes are bloodied and his grin is a feral white slice across his face. He brandishes a steel bat, hair and gore staining its length. He dips his chin and points the length of the bloodied weapon at Vela.

"I'm cleansing this town."

"Whose blood is on that bat?" I ask. "The Meshed don't bleed."

"No," says Jonkirk, "but sinners do."

Vela blanches. She clutches the child tighter and backs toward the rear wall. I swoop and pick up the laser cutter, stepping in front to defend her.

Amos steps in next to me. "Stay away from us, Priest!" he growls.

Jonkirk throws his head back, brow glistening with the fervour of madness. "It's much too late for that."

He lifts his hand and from behind him, three Meshed appear, death-mask faces grim. Their corroded casings and dead flesh, sunken and coloured like half-rotten peaches, tells the story of a species in as much decline as we humans are.

I brandish the cutter higher. It seems such a small, ineffectual weapon in the face of superior strength. The ignited tip glitters like a brilliant diamond.

"You let them in, didn't you, Jonkirk?" whispers Vela. "You are letting them kill all the women."

The priest sneers at her. He pulls the front of his robe down. His chest is revealed, plate metal sheets over his lungs and heart.

"You are one of *them*?" I whisper, horrified.

"I've *embraced* them."

"Traitor," I snarl, my stomach soured and the cutter slipping in my sweaty palm.

"No," says Jonkirk. "The Meshed are the gods' new children." His eyes slip to the baby in Vela's grasp, "And unlike you they *give* life to the world."

My heart twists and Vela blanches.

"Their technology," he continues, "renders you redundant. Children are now birthed from machines and like cancer, mothers will be cut from the world. Boys will be raised to flourish in this new environment. I will create a utopian society, forged on a foundation of strength."

"And what of the girl children?"

"To be disposed of." He nods at Sonya's corpse. "That one knew it carried a girl. That's why it ran.

Why it was stupid enough to seek sanctuary here, I don't know."

Horror wars with my rage. "You'll turn this world into a battlefield."

"It already is one."

Jonkirk lowers the bat, half turning to the waiting Meshed. "Time to end this. Kill them," he commands. "The baby also."

The three machine-men surge forward, heavy boots hitting the floor like hammers to an anvil.

Time seems to slow. I smell the oil in their joints, the sweet rot scent of their flesh parts, and the traces of man-made chemical winds on their exoskeleton skins.

Amos unholsters his blaster and fires. The first Meshed thuds to the floor, head disintegrated. Amos swivels and the second machine reels back with a cry, chest opened and spraying thin, red oil.

But the third clenches him around the torso. It squeezes and Amos gasps as his ribs crack like deadwood. He coughs and blood sprays across his chest, the bright red that comes from crushed lungs.

"Run," he chokes on his fluid-filled throat.

I throw the cutter aside, grasp Vela's arm and shove her and the baby toward the exit. The child squeals at the sudden jostle. The remaining Meshed swings a heavy arm at my head and I skid sideways to avoid the blow. My boots slide on loose metal shavings and I cry out as I fall heavily to my hip. Vela stumbles behind, but somehow holds herself upright. She races for the exit but Jonkirk, quicker, catches her around the waist. She falls against him and he tears the baby from her arms. Then he shoves her away, stepping back whilst holding the child up by its arm.

The baby screams, face red and puckered...

"NO!" Vela sobs.

The last Meshed looms over me and I lose sight of the others. I stare up into his soulless eyes. "You don't have to do this."

"I do what I must," he replies.

"And so do I!" cracks a familiar voice.

Metal hands curl around my attacker's neck. In a spray of sparks, his head is twisted to the left. His body topples sideways, replaced by Sonya's grim features.

"I've a few amps left in the battery," she says.

I nod, relieved, and Sonya turns. Jonkirk is stone as he stares her down.

"Hand me my daughter," demands Sonya.

Jonkirk lifts the squealing baby higher.

"Do it or you will be dead before you hit the floor."

"You are almost done, Meshed. You won't make it."

"No?" Sonya glances across his shoulder.

Vela stands there, a steel bar in hand. With a grunt, she swings and strikes Jonkirk in the abdomen. He doubles over and Vela snatches the baby from his nerveless grip. The priest crumples to his knees. Two jerky steps and Sonya reaches him.

"I heard your sermon from my cell," she says. "Your history is wrong, Priest. Women were always the warriors. It was our children sent to slaughter—our children who died screaming as they drowned in mud and blood. It's far harder to lose a child and be consumed by grief, than to die for any gods you may worship."

Sonya reaches down and tears open the front of Jonkirk's robe. His retrofitted chestplate is torn out, followed by his exposed mechanical heart. Jonkirk shudders and falls still.

Sonya collapses to her knees.

She is silent for a moment then extends her arms. "Please. Let me hold her just once."

Vela circles the corpses littering the floor and for the first time in thirty years, hands a new mother her baby.

The ghost of a smile plays across Sonya's lips.

"I'm shutting down, little one," she says to the girl. "I'm sorry I won't see you grow." Her voice box crackles then resolves. "But I name you Hope, for that is what this world needs."

Her eyes never leave her baby, but the tone of her voice changes—these next words meant for us. "There's a hidden facility, six kilometres north from here, out past the wastelands. That's where I was headed. Everything you need is there. Food, shelter, clean air and water. Other Meshed mothers also. Take my daughter there. Tell them I sent you. My sisters will help and protect you."

Sonya's head dips and her hands grow lax. A low internal alarm sounds out, cut short as her components fail.

Vela gently lifts the baby clear. She holds her close. "We need to find that facility," she says.

"We?"

"Yes."

"Why 'we'?"

Vela's eyes gleam. "I fix humans, you fix machines. Can't you see your value in a place like that?"

Outside, the fervour of the initial fighting has dimmed, replaced with the marching cadence of metal boots on flagstones. Soon the other Meshed will find us.

"We won't make the gate," I say.

Vela touches the baby's cheek. "We can try."

"But we've no weapons."

"No, but I'm guessing that car of yours is pretty fast."

I glance at the Venom and press my lips together.

"I'll get the keys."

Vela nods and outside, the bell begins to toll.

PASSENGER

Amsterdam to Heathrow Flight

I thought I was ready. But I'm not. Not really. Flying passenger class in a plane under clear skies is one thing, but strapped in riding the back of a storm is quite another. Lightning. Turbulence. The crying of a baby and the smell of fear from the woman sitting next to me. They are triggering my responses. I suck in a stabilising breath. I'd be a lot better up in the cockpit. In control. But I'm not permitted to fly until I prove to Her Majesty's Royal Armed Forces that I've recovered. I clench my teeth and grip my seat tighter. My fingernails press into the worn leather. British RAF pilot, Alex Logan—that's me—Mr Fucked Up In The Head ever since the last covert ops I undertook with Special Forces in Syria went wrong.

I lean back and focus on the small details around me, the smell of the recirculated air, the flickering images of the TV show—re-runs of *The Fresh Prince of Bel-Air*—playing on my neighbour's iPad screen. But it doesn't help. All I keep thinking about is how I lost my wings that day over Syria—how I fell from the sky, losing both my plane and best friend, Connor Johns, in a hail of ISIS militant fire.

"Oh c'mon, Alex," says Connor. "Don't be so melodramatic. You need to let this go. You didn't kill me. *They* did."

I glance to my left. Connor stands in the aisle. His pilot's uniform clings slick to his skin, soaked in blood. The left half of his face is missing. The man sitting across and just behind me—a bald, bearded man with glasses—is visible through my friend's transparent body.

I turn back. Connor isn't really here. He's dead. The plane suddenly drops as the crosswinds outside shift. My seatbelt constricts around my waist.

He's dead. He's dead. He's dead.

The view of the cabin suddenly shifts, changing from a dimly lit, people-filled space into a day from my past—a blistering day in a far away desert filled with fire, smoke, blood and sand. I blink, pushing the flashback away. Connor died there in the shadow of our plane's ruptured wing with a punctured chest and his face torn away. I tried to revive him. I still taste his blood on my lips.

This is a different plane. Syria is far away.

"Hey Alex. Look at the sky," says Connor, his voice rasping.

I know I should ignore him, but don't. I turn my head. The porthole window offers a small glimpse of broken clouds, lightning skittering along their skirts—silver against dread grey. Once I would have thought it beautiful. But I don't find joy in much of anything anymore.

Not even the black-haired air hostess who stops with her drinks cart next to me.

"Can I get you anything, sir?" she asks. I'm stuck by how her blood-red fingernails are an exact shade to match her painted lips. And those lips—the way they smile—just a little more than professional friendliness. I'm pretty sure she would give me her number if I asked for it.

"Sir, are you okay?" she asks again. Her blue eyes remind me of desert skies.

"Ah, yes," I manage to say. Connor grins. "Just water, thanks."

"No problem." The woman reaches through Connor's transparent chest and into her drinks cart. The clear water bottle she places on my tray table drips with condensation.

"You should definitely get her number," says Connor, his gaze following the air hostess as she moves further along the aisle.

My ex-girlfriend, Alice's voice muscles into my head. "You're seriously screwed up, Alex. I'm leaving. And do womankind a favour and don't go inflicting your fucked-up self on any other poor unsuspecting girl."

I frown and unscrew the lid of the water bottle. The liquid burns cold as it slides down my throat.

"Alice was a bitch," says Connor. He leans his elbow on the backrest of my seat. Phantom blood dribbles from his sleeve onto the floor.

"Shut up," I mutter. Alice was well within her rights to leave me.

"Excuse me?" says the woman sitting next to me. "Were you talking to me?"

I shake my head and tip my chin, pretending it's about the people in the seat behind us.

The two men. The woman nods knowingly and turns back to her iPad. The men's voices have been an annoying litany for the entire flight. I listen as their current topic of conversation leaks in through the crack between the seats.

"Have you heard about the virus breakout? Some governments are apparently enforcing full lock down. Crazy shit like shooting people in the street."

"Yeah. But you never can tell the truth of those stories. They wouldn't just kill people for no reason."

"No reason? You are so fucking naïve. This virus is spreading. People are dying over there. I saw it on the news, they didn't show bodies but whole complexes were being barricaded to keep the sick out—or in maybe, I don't know. But it looked bad. You can't tell me they aren't afraid."

"Well hopefully they'll find a cure. It's just flu symptoms right? The old and young are at risk, but you know, more people die of cancer every day."

"True, but I got a friend who works in virus research. He reckons things like this tend to mutate— you know, get real bad, real quick…"

I've heard enough. I've got more important things to worry about than a virus infecting people half way across the world. I unclip my belt and stand. The air hostess has the aisle blocked down the back, but the path to the toilets at the front of the cabin is clear. I step out, gripping the headrest. The man sitting on the aisle opposite me stands up suddenly.

His tray table is covered in beer cans, another one is held in his fist. Sweat slicks his brow. He frowns as he leans into the aisle—a clear challenge. But while he towers over me, he is slimmer in build. I know I could take him if he wants to start something. I don't move back, but instead slowly lift my chin to lock gazes with him. A challenge of my own. But Connor growls low at my back. A warning. I take note. He was always smarter at picking fights than me. I smooth out my features and place my hand out, palm up.

"After you," I say. The man glares at me for a moment longer, and then steps out. As he does, he stumbles and the beer in his hand slops over me. He clutches his chest and coughs, beer-tainted spittle sprays across my face. He coughs again. This time the wet sound is followed by a slew of vomit that shoots across his chin and over my boots.

"For fuck's sake," I snarl stepping back from him. I wipe the back of my palm across my face in disgust. My boots are beyond salvaging.

The man grins weakly. "Hostess won't think you're so pretty now."

"Hit the fucker!" whispers Connor in my ear.

But I'm not fighting anyone while covered in puke. "Get out of my way," I say.

The man wipes his mouth. "Look, sorry. Air sickness and a few too many brews. I didn't mean anything by it."

The hostess minus her trolley arrives, her hands full of napkins. "Please gentlemen. Move aside. Let's get this mess cleaned up."

She's smiling, but the tightness of her lips betrays her disgust. The sick man nods, but then doubles over and coughs again. Before the hostess can move, her shirt is sprayed with more vomit.

I'll give her credit. She looks like she is about to gag, but doesn't. A consummate professional.

"Oh shit, I'm sorry, love," murmurs the sick man, trying to pat her blouse clean.

"Please," says the hostess, pushing his hands away. She reaches past him and pulls an airsick bag from the seatback. "Take this and sit down."

The passenger complies. I feel sorry for the woman as she kneels down and starts to clean. She glances at me as I squeeze past her, heading for the toilets. No smile on her face this time.

There is someone already in the cubicle. I curse. Behind the closed door, a cough barks out. Then a rushing swoosh as the bowl is evacuated and the gentle gurgle of water in the sink. The door clicks open. A young woman steps out. Her hand rests for a moment on the door handle. "All yours," she mutters, blowing her nose on a tissue as she passes. I notice a small smear of blood on the tissue as she folds it away. Jesus. Is everyone on this flight goddamn sick?

I step in and pull the door shut. The handle is still moist from the woman's grip. I turn the tap on and scrub my face. I feel marginally better. I kick off my boots and tip the toe of the first under the tap. Chunks of vomit slide away from the black patent leather, falling to clog up the drain. I poke at the mess with a paper towel. It jerks thickly past the drain and down into the pipe. Fucking disgusting.

I drop my shoes, rinse my hands again and rest both palms on the bench. I take a deep breath. My reflection glares back at me from the mirror—my sandy-blond hair in its military cut, grey eyes and a week's facial growth. Even I can tell I look tired. Just a little while longer and we'll land. Then I can rest and finally get back to work.

All will be good.

"We both know you aren't good." Connor appears behind me, his reflection staring at me from the mirror.

"Leave me alone," I mutter.

"You know I'm not really here so I can't technically leave you alone."

"Jesus. I just want to go to the toilet in peace."

"Fine. I'll wait outside. But we need to have this discussion. You can't go back to work while still having hallucinations like this. You'll end up killing yourself or someone else."

I swallow. Connor's right, or maybe it's my conscience talking. But the problem is, I can't stay off work like this anymore, either. It's a slippery slope to hell if I have to spend much more time twiddling my thumbs on forced medical leave. I need my next meeting with the base psychologist to go well. She needs to clear me this time round.

I just want to get back. I'll be okay once I'm in the pilot seat again.

"That's if they ever let you back in a plane," says Connor. "Trust me. They'll work out what's going on with you."

"No they WON'T!" My anger peaks. I punch the mirror. The glass splinters, erasing the ghostly image of Connor's face.

"Doing that just proves my point," says Connor's voice, now disembodied. "Your fucked if you go ahead with this review."

"Don't worry. I'm ready." I slowly reach down to turn the tap on. The blood welling on my knuckles slides away in the cool current of water. Outside the intercom address system activates.

"Please fasten your seat belts and lift your trays into the upright position. Crew, prepare the cabin for landing."

I pull a clean paper towel out and wrap it over the cuts. I push open the door and head back to my seat.

Connor is already there, waiting, when I get back.

***

John Radcliffe Hospital, Oxford, UK

The meeting with the psychologist didn't go to plan. But to be fair, I went in not feeling the greatest—both feverish and lethargic and with intermittent nosebleeds. Then the woman confirmed she wouldn't be re-instating me to active duty at this time. I lost it and punched a wall. Security arrived and indelicately restrained me with a kick to the guts. Not my finest moment.

And now I've been admitted.

And I feel like shit.

The Defence Hospital Unit at the John Radcliffe Hospital isn't so bad. I've been given my own room, spacious and painted in calming shades of green. The window opposite my bed overlooks the car park and the hospital's emergency helipad just beyond. A helicopter landed five minutes ago. It still sits there mocking me—the pilot's seat within representing everything I want and all I can't have.

One thing I do still have is Connor. He haunts me, sitting in the chair by my bed. But I'm glad for his company. Without family here in England I'm alone, and this sickness has got me scared.

I cough and my lungs clench around a ball of razor-blade pains. I press my fist to my chest until it eases. My arm feels heavy.

"You really do look like shit," says Connor.

I clear my throat. A ball of mucous slides up into my mouth. I spit into a tissue and frown at the blood streaking it. "I really do feel like shit."

Nurse Smith walks into my room. I can't tell if she's pretty or not due to the green facemask she always wears. She stalks over to the drip and taps the clear tube leading to the cannula in my arm.

Behind her arrives Doctor Williams, his face also masked. Tall and lithe, he moves to my bedside, graceful for a fifty-something-year-old man. "Morning Alex," he says.

"Morning."

He looks tired. "I'm afraid it's bad news," he says. "Tests have come back confirming a mutated strain of coronavirus. A particularly aggressive one."

"You'll beat it," whispers Connor.

"So how long will I be down?" I ask.

Doctor Williams frowns. "We can't say for sure. It's a mutated strain. Highly aggressive. Our priority will be to stabilise your respiratory system until it can heal."

If it heals. The words hang unspoken in the air. I bite my lip. My lungs are a constant pain in my chest, and it's growing worse. The urge to cough overtakes again. I cover my mouth, but it comes with more force than I expect. Blood splatters hot across my palm and sprays past my fingers. Flecks mar the doctor's facemask.

Horrified, I squint up at him. "I'm so sorry…" I start to say.

The doctor's eyes are wide, but he remains calm. "It's okay. I'm okay." He gently presses me back to my pillow. My limbs, weak with fever, give way. I collapse backward.

"We'll do our best to make you comfortable." He glances up at the nurse. "A dose of morphine and Temazepam to help him sleep."

The doctor turns back to me. He pats me on the arm. "Don't worry, son, we'll have you back up and about as soon as we can."

Connor stands and glares at the doctor. "You better bloody well do so," he snarls. "It's not his turn to die yet."

***

I wake, woozy. My mouth tastes like old blood and my lungs are two pools of fire in my chest. It's dark both in my room and outside the window. I search for Connor. He's there, pacing by the exit door. His eyes are glued to the small viewing panel that looks out into the corridor. He must sense me. He turns. His ruined face is revealed, half cast in shadow and half in the blue-white flickering lights slipping in through the glass in the door. His lips press thin.

"What's happening?" I ask.

"Go back to sleep, Alex," he says.

"Why?"

"It's not good out there."

"Is that gunfire I hear?"

Connor stalks to my bed. "Don't worry about anything, Alex," he says. "I'm here. I'll watch over you."

I'm so tired. I close my eyes and do as he says. Darkness welcomes me with open arms.

***

A beeping alarm pulls me from sleep. The drip must be empty. My eyes, crusted with sleep and sickness, sting as I blink, struggling to make out the details of my darkened room. It's stuffy in here. I can barely breathe. Who turned the air-con off? And I really need to take a piss. I ease myself up from my pillow. The door to the ensuite is close but it may as well be a thousand kilometres away.

I press the nurse-call buzzer and it buzzes outside. I wait a full three minutes but no one comes. Where are they? Looks like I'm going to have to make my own way to the toilet.

I peel back my blankets and swing my feet over the side of the bed. My vision swims. I suppress the urge to vomit and grip the mobile frame of the drip, using it to lever myself up. The vinyl floor leaches cold into my heels. I stand swaying for a moment and then shuffle towards the bathroom.

Connor appears at my side. "That's right, just one step at a time. Focus on your feet."

"Where is everybody?" I ask, eyes fixed on the bathroom.

Connor glances at the exit door, then back. "Just get to the toilet," he says. "We don't want you to make a mess out here."

It's a relief to reach the bowl. Connor gives me my privacy as I work to adjust my hospital gown, his back to me as he hovers by the door.

"We need to find a way to get you out of here," he says.

"I'm still sick." I finish. The toilet flushes with a harsh gurgle. I grip the drip frame like it's my only lifeline.

"The situation's changed." He glances at me. "Think you are up to flying? Can you make it to the helipad? It's about a hundred metres away, across the car park."

My vision swims. "I crashed the last helicopter I flew," I say thinking back to my uncle's cattle property in Australia, near Darwin.

"That's 'cause you're a shit pilot." The ghost of a smile touches his ruined lips. "Seriously though. You got the strength to do it?"

My lungs still hurt. My throat and nose are clogged with mucus and clotted blood. But the fever is down. I nod. "I could if I needed too."

"You need to," says Connor.

Death has lent Connor a certain, unsettling gravity. He's different to the jovial man he was in life. A chill crawls down my spine. Hallucination or not, I decide to trust him.

The door to my room opens out into chaos—a scene cut straight from a horror movie. Fluorescent lights flicker in the grid ceilings. On and off, punctuating flash-point images of the corridor and nurse station. Trolleys lay toppled, their cargos of multi-coloured medications and paper cups spilled out like confetti. Blood and various body fluids stain walls and floors, a miasma of stench rising from it all. I gag and press my sleeve to my nose. *Fuck. What the hell happened here?*

A trail of blood smears the pale green vinyl floor. The streaked blade of scarlet leads into the nurse station.

It's there I find the first body.

Nurse Smith.

She lies face up, eyes open, on the floor in the centre of the room. Her mask has slipped askew, revealing lips blackened in death. A sheet of paper lies next to her lax hand. I lean in. It's a fax. A government logo glares at me from the top left corner. Black letters dance before my eyes.

We hereby advise that John Radcliffe Hospital is to quarantine due to a viral outbreak. All patients and staff are to be secured within the building.
Any persons breaching quarantine orders will be shot on sight.

A sudden urge to escape the hospital's confines consumes me. I've never been one for being caged. With the nurse beyond my help I shuffle further down the hall, still gripping the frame but moving faster now. Connor stalks ahead of me, his boots eerily silent as they pound the floor. He checks the rooms, left to right. Always the soldier.

More bodies line the corridor, sprawled in various states of decomposition. I pass one man, a patient by the look of his gown, huddled in a corner, fists clutched to his chest and face bloodied to his chin. Three more nurses are crumpled on the floor by the coffee machine in the small dining area, corpses—black and bloated—starting to stink.

My training keeps me calm on the surface, but somewhere deep in my chest, my heart batters uneasy against my ribs. If I leave the hospital will I be shot? I cough and cough again, but then realise it's not a cough at all. It's a sob.

I don't want to die. I didn't want to die in Syria. I definitely don't want it to end here.

"Steady mate," whispers Connor, his voice sounding far away. "We'll get you out of here."

"Why are you helping me? I failed you. You died because of me!"

"No, Alex. I died because it was my time. Keep going. Follow my voice."

But it's hard. Each step is like wading through concrete...

"Get up Alex!"

I don't remember hitting the floor. But here I am with the drip frame fallen across my legs. I taste vomit at the back of my throat.

"Get up NOW!"

"I hate you, Connor," I snarl. Pushing myself up, I hobble forward. The exit is close, with the grey light of dawn filtering in through the glazed main entrance doors.

One step.

Two steps.

The helipad is a beacon across the car park. A helicopter sits, waiting.

Freedom.

Connor stands by the door. His eyes lock onto mine. "We get to the helicopter. You get inside, start it and then head hell-for-leather out of town."

"Why is a helicopter even here?" I ask. It seems all too convenient.

Connor frowns. "Pilot got trapped here in the lockdown. He tried to leave but didn't make it."

I glance back at the helipad. This time I notice the helicopter's cockpit door hanging half open, the bullet-riddled windshield and a corpse slumped in the pilot's seat.

The world spins. Grey into white into black. I cough again. I can't do this. I'm not going to make it.

"Fucking man up," says Connor, "and get your arse to that chopper. Get there or die here. You're the last one alive in this place. There's no one left to help you."

And I know he's right. This building is a tomb. I grit my teeth. The auto entry door slides open on my approach. A blast of cold, English air brushes over my face. Just got to get to the helicopter. I take a deep breath.

"I'm right by your side," whispers Connor.

I run.

My bare feet slap the concrete of the helipad just as the sound of gunfire erupts.

I fall.

Connor screams at me, "GET UP!"

I want to. I really do. But I'm done.

Connor snarls. His ice-cold hands grip me around my shoulders and I cry out in pain. It's like he is tearing my soul from my bones. But in moments he has me upright and again running for the helicopter.

I'm not sure how I do, but I make it. I pull the corpse free of the seat and let it slither to the ground. I scramble into the cockpit. My breaths are fire in my lungs; my heart threatens to explode. I activate the ignition and rotors amidst another hail of gunfire.

The helicopter lifts uncertainly into the air. I grin at Connor, now sitting in the co-pilot seat. But he doesn't grin back.

"Head for the coast," he says.

I nod and take one last glance down at the hospital with its military quarantine barricades and armed forces in Hazmat suits that service it.

I'm out of here.

My whole body hurts, but the *whoop, whoop* of the helicopter's blades is comforting. I push the stick and turn, heading for London and the coast.

Everything is better now I'm in the cockpit and in control.

***

London city emerges on the horizon, cloaked in a miasma of shifting smoke. As we draw closer, details refine. Charred buildings border ruined streets that are either barricaded or on fire. Ant-like figures dart desperately from one set of cover to the next. By Westminster Palace, the Thames runs thick with rubbish—cars, cruise boats with their backs broken, and bodies.

I swallow, sickened by more than just the virus. In the nursery rhyme it's London Bridge that's said to fall, but here and now, in reality, London herself has collapsed—the once-queen of cities, stripped of her jewels and her dignity.

Connor leans forward in his seat.

"Holy hell," he says. "What's the world come to?"

"I don't know. But we've gotta out of here." I glance at the fuel gauge, trying to ignore the taste of blood at the back of my throat. "Tanks are full. We should be able to make it to Calais. Maybe things are different there."

"Or maybe not," mutters Connor, his eyes fixed to the laid-bare corpse of London.

The helicopter rises. Big Ben emerges from the smoke, the clock's turret a black spire against the grey backdrop. Its hands point to ten and six—mid-morning.

Plenty of daylight to make the trip.

I push the stick. The helicopter dips left on cue but a hissing sound catches my attention, swallowing the drone of the rotor blades. My stomach drops. It's a sound I know all too well.

A sound I heard over Syria.

A sound Connor recognises as well.

"Brace for impact!" he screams.

A ground-to-air missile, fired from within the palace barricade, collides with the midsection of the helicopter. The stick is torn from my hand. Metal tears with a whine and the aircraft's nose dips sickeningly. We spin.

The cabin is filled with smoke and heat prickles the back of my neck. Alarms blare. "Fuck!" I scream, fighting to right and hold the craft on an even keel.

But it's no good. This isn't Syria.

There's no landing for me this time.

Big Ben looms close, its face a single white eye. The helicopter, as if taking offence, ploughs into it—through it.

Fire, heat, the shear of metal and the roar of crumbling masonry.

***

The street is solid beneath my feet. Around me lie the scattered parts of a helicopter. There is a corpse too, bloodied and broken, sprawled face down on the bitumen. The muscled form with its blond hair and hospital gown seem familiar.

"Don't look," says Connor. "You can't change it. We just move forward from here."

"That's my body, isn't it? I'm dead?"

Connor presses his hand to my torn chest. His touch is warm this time.

"We are here together."

"That's not an answer."

"You don't need me to answer."

"But I don't want to move forward," I say.

Connor sighs. "It's a hell of a lot better than moving back."

I glance again at my own corpse. He's right.

Whatever this is—death, life, half-life—it's better than the wreck of what is left behind.

"C'mon," says Connor, squeezing my shoulder. "Let's find another plane and get out of here."

Yes. That's all I really want.

To be back in the pilot's seat again.

Back in the cockpit and in control.

THESE MANY DEAD MEN

Kent Rhys

F ive men line the back wall of my cell. Watery afternoon sunlight filters in from the window, slicing through their translucent bodies. Clad only in hospital gowns, their shoulders tremble, and their eyes, black pits to hell, stare, accusing.

You did this to us, Kent Rhys.

Yes. Yes I did.

I turn away from the haunts and back to my journal. I rub a hand across my eyes, and then press the pencil to the paper. It scratches across the yellowed page.

I deserve to be where I am.

I deserve to pay penance for my sins.

Redemption comes in saving Thomas.

Thomas Norris. He shifts in his cell, muttering and cursing beneath his breath. He punches the barred door that separates us and I flinch. I'll not respond to his call for attention. He's been my patient for some years now. He is the reason I came to this facility, my hope being that in saving him I can atone for the old blood that stains my hands. But I'm not sure if I am helping him. He is always angry—holding delusions that the government implants what he calls 'chips' into his arms, to monitor and control him.

But I *was* government. And it was never about restraint. The tests I conducted as an army psychiatrist on soldiers like Thomas were about stopping the bloodshed. We wanted to use hallucinogenic drugs to confuse and disorientate rather than allow the further slaughter of young men.

I didn't know at the time that one weapon was just as brutal as the other.

I glance down at the crisscross scars that mark my forearms. Thomas has attacked me many times. He has an unquiet mind, brutal and savage.

My patient is not a gentle man.

***

Thomas Norris

The doc snuffles and sniffles in his cell. I consider him through the barred door. Just a sick-looking old man. Pathetic. They say he killed five men in his time. I can't see how. He's too soft. There's no real soldier in him.

But he reckons it's true. Said he meant well and that it was accidental. A bad batch of drugs injected in a bid to take the fighting spirit out of them. It stopped their hearts. He sickens me. And it's not because the men died, but that the doc is a fucking pacifist. Soldiers are made for war and blood and gore. What's the point of having us, if they don't want us to actually fight?

Well that's what I think.

I punch the bars of the door, and the doc flinches. He doesn't look at me. I grit my teeth, grinding them together—bone on bone. Blood drips from my knuckles. My attention turns to the five ghosts that line the back wall of the doc's cell. I've not seen a more pissed-off looking bunch of cobbers.

I get it. They were murdered. They deserve to be angry. So, I salute them. Blood tracks down my wrist. The smell reminds me of guns in my hand and the roar of war.

The ghosts don't salute back.

I turn and settle back on the bed. My ragged journal lies open on the pillow, its pages brimming with words the doc encourages me to write—words that stab and spill out my rage. Next to it rests my pencil. I consider its slender length. The tip is not the slicing edge I wish for, but it could do the job. I pick it up. The doc won't like this, but it must be done. I hold the pencil's tip to the inside of my arm. Sharpened recently against the concrete wall, the graphite glistens, scalpel sharp. I press it to my scarred skin and push. Blood wells. Thick. Warm. I scrape deeper and the flesh parts with a sting. I welcome the pain. It confirms I hold a measure of control. My life does not belong to the government.

The pencil falls to the open journal. Scarlet stains the page. I turn my arm to the filtered light coming in from the barred window. My nails, ingrained with dirt, scrape at the wound. A glint of silver. I dig and the edge of the metal catches. I flick it out. It falls to the floor with a small *clink*.

Anyone else will tell you it is shrapnel. But that's not the truth.

It's a control chip.

***

Kent Rhys

The sun's passed, moved on to wherever it slumbers when night approaches. I hate the late hours in this building. Hamer House Hospice is full of sorrow— the bricks and mortar soaked in it. The rooms in this basement ward are worse than most. I know I should ask for a better space from which to work, as it is miserable here. The damp leaches into everything. But I'll not go anywhere. I won't leave Thomas. He needs me. Only this evening he attacked again, cutting my arm open as punishment for not giving him the freedom he thinks he deserves.

Freedom he is too dangerous to be granted.

But it's also the night nurse, Arthur, that convinces me to stay. Not a bad man on the whole, but he's not sensitive to the needs of those suffering from mental trauma.

People like Thomas.

The moans of the other poor souls who inhabit the ward filter into my room. Over them, I hear footsteps and the familiar jangle of keys.

Arthur.

His shadow fills the viewing panel in my door. A key slithers into the lock. *Click*. The door swings open and light spills in across the floor. I squint.

Arthur's voice scrapes into the room. "Kent? Or is it Thomas?"

My eyes adjust, and the night nurse's dark features solidify. My gaze slips past the line of gnarled flesh that gleams beneath his left ear. That's the mark of the butcher, Robert, who dwells in Cell 1. A man more animal than human. Rumour is he once attacked Arthur—tried to cut his face off. I ignore the scar. Past experience has taught me not to linger on it or ask questions.

"It's okay. Thomas is in his cell. It's safe," I say.

Arthur nods and slips into the room. On rare occasions, and only ever in the dead of night, he comes to talk to the psychiatrist in me—comes to seek insight when his job gets too hard. Such has our relationship always been defined. He is the keeper of the patients and I, the keeper of his secrets.

Arthur closes the door and leans against the frame. He carries no weapon other than his hands. He needs no others. Those fists are all power.

"I'm getting old, Doc." Arthur glances at the viewing panel, and back. "And so are you. We've both been here a while."

"Yes," I say. "But we do good work here. Looking after our patients is not an easy job."

Arthur grimaces. His teeth glitter white. "You don't have any patients, Kent. Remember? You're as batshit crazy as the rest of those in this zoo."

I swallow the comment's sting. "If wanting to help a man makes me crazy, then I must live with that."

Arthur shakes his head and presses his thumb and pointer finger to the bridge of his nose. His hand drops. "How many times do I have to tell you? Thomas doesn't exist. He is in your head."

My five ghosts appear again along the back wall. They crowd forward, fingers plucking at my nightshirt. I clench my teeth.

"Thomas is real."

Arthur shakes his head. "I wish you could be made to see the truth."

"Others have tried." A memory flares briefly of pads against my temples, a rag in my mouth and electricity scorching through my brain. Electroconvulsive therapy.

Arthur shifts, uncomfortably. He's aware of those treatments. He was the one to nurse me back. His lips press thin.

"Okay then. So let's pretend Thomas is real," he says. "What will you do, Doc, when you work out you can't save him? What happens when you realise you are a fucking zookeeper and the people you are trying to help would all be better off dead?"

And so the reason for his visit is revealed. Arthur is struggling to find the point of being here at all. I can't say I blame him. The cells he tends are filled with monsters.

I weave calm into my voice. "Would you rather see your patients dead, Arthur? Trust me, I've been there. I do not recommend it, even for a man with character as strong as yours."

The nurse's dark eyes dance. In that moment I know merciful murder is on his mind. Then his shoulders slump.

"Nah, Doc. Just feeling worn out is all. Been too long at this thankless job."

He turns to go and as his form disappears through my door, Thomas whispers from his cell.

"He'd do it you know. That bastard is as crazy as the rest of us."

I bite my lip.

***

Thomas Norris

Old Charlie died last night. Rumour is he chewed off his own tongue and drowned in the blood. Sounds bad, but he did worse to his victims. A karmic death I reckon. Arthur's now cleaning out the cell, shoulders hunched. The air stinks of bleach.

"You'd make some woman a lovely housewife, Arty," I say.

The nurse glances at me. His depthless gaze bores through me. I recall his conversation last night with Kent and I wonder if maybe Arthur himself killed Charlie—held him down with a pillow 'til he bit his own tongue off trying to get a breath.

"And you'll never have a wife, Thomas," he replies.

I sneer. What the fuck do I care about women when I have the bloody government breathing down my neck? I scratch my arm and find yet another lump under my skin. They must have managed to get another chip in last night while I slept. I'm sick of them coming for me, for using their hush-hush science to control me. They want me silenced. And the chips are their weapons.

I close my eyes and take a breath.

My life does not belong to the government.

***

Kent Rhys

I saw Charlie's body as it was wheeled away, his skeletal hand hanging lax from beneath a bloodstained sheet. I muttered a prayer for him as he passed, knowing his body would not be honoured. The best any like him can expect is dismemberment by medical students looking to learn. A broken brain is considered by many doctors to be an interesting brain.

Night shift has just started. Arthur's voice reverberates down the corridor, lending weight to the atmosphere. He's speaking with the woman called Parrot in her cell. I can't quite make out the words. I lean in against the door, straining to hear.

Something about a new addition to the ward.

Patient or nurse?

Ah. A new nurse it seems.

Arthur's late night visit makes new sense. He is retiring. Or is being replaced. A good thing really. His time here has damaged him.

The zookeeper wants the animals dead…

I lie down on my bed, slipping my journal beneath my pillow. It contains my notes on my last conversation with Thomas. The soldier was agitated today. He claims a new chip has been put into his arm. I couldn't feel it there and wrestled away the sharpened spoon handle he intended to cut himself with. But he took his measure of blood. He cut me again and deep this time. The day shift had to stitch my wound. I close my eyes and try to sleep. My arm aches. I do not relish the pain of it.

***

Thomas Norris

I pace by the door. I didn't mean to hurt the doc—didn't mean to slice his arm open. He may be weak, but as a soldier, it's my job to protect the weak, right? That's what we do. But he shouldn't have tried to stop me. The chips under my skin need to be removed.

I glance at him. He sleeps face up, his breaths irregular. His fingers twitch on his chest. Nightmares again no doubt. The ghosts stand silent by his bed. Tonight their eyes leak blood. The doc cries out and then turns to face the wall. I make a promise to myself to try and be gentler with the doctor in the future. I guess we can't all be warriors.

***

Kent Rhys

Arthur's hollering out in the corridor wakens me. He's cursing and cussing. I roll off my bed, ignoring the ghosts standing to the side. Tonight they are all wearing Thomas's face. Strange.

Barefoot, I ease my way to the viewing panel in the door. My long nightshirt flaps around my thighs. I look out onto carnage. Arthur is in the open storage cell across the way, nursing a bloodied hand. The lines of his face are pinched tight with pain and rage. Parrot is screeching in her cell, a wild cackle that sets my hair on end. A youngish man, brown-haired and slight-framed, bends over a trolley, picking up spilled medications. Must be the new nurse.

Arthur points and yells, "Drew, the keys!"

I don't hear what else Arthur says next. As the new nurse turns, I catch a glimpse of his face. My stomach drops. He's aged a little, but that pointed chin and slim nose—I'd recognise them anywhere. Those features haunt my nightmares every night.

He was the fifth to die.

Of the soldiers I killed.

Drew?

I stumble back a step.

How can it be?

It can't be.

Drew is dead.

Then he sees me too. His shoulders tense and the baby-like lines of his chin harden.

In slow motion, the boy turns away from my cell. He heads towards the storage cell instead—toward Arthur. The old nurse stumbles back with a curse as Drew pushes him into the room.

The bitter clang of the closing door sounds like a death knell.

Arthur's trapped.

Parrot laughs louder.

My ghosts gather closer around me, leering.

You are a dead man, Kent Rhys.

***

<u>Thomas Norris</u>

The doc is huddled on his bed, sheet skewed around his thin, dirty ankles. His eyes are wide, shifting from side to side. I would have thought him used to seeing ghosts. Perhaps it's different when your ghosts are actually breathing.

The new nurse enters the doc's cell. Drew, I assume. He leaves the door open. Yellow light, the colour of old vomit, cuts into the room.

Old Arthur is hollering from the locked cell across the way. "What the hell are you doing, Drew! Close that door!"

A smart boy would definitely have closed the door.

Drew doesn't look all that smart to me.

"Doctor Kent Rhys," says the nurse in a slow, wicked drawl. "Remember me?"

The doc doesn't answer.

"Well, I can't say I'm pleased to see you either." Drew tilts his head, a crazy glint catching in the white of his eye. "Or perhaps I am…"

"But...but...you are dead! YOU ARE DEAD!" screeches Kent.

Doc's lost his mind, it seems.

Kent's fingers flutter against the sheet. He crouches in closer to the wall. His pillow shifts and the corner of his journal slips out from beneath it.

"I'm far from dead, no thanks to you," says Drew. He paces further into the cell. The doc's ghosts mill around him. I note now that there are only four.

"But how?" mutters Kent, eyes wide. "I saw you die. I saw them wrap your body."

Drew frowns. "Pity you didn't stick around. I woke up a few hours later in the morgue." He pulls down the collar of his shirt to reveal a long thin scar running from his collarbone toward his heart. "Just as they started the cut to autopsy me."

The doc looks sick. He reaches out, fingers thin and stained with dirt and the graphite from his pencils. "I am so sorry, my boy."

"You don't get to apologise," snarls Drew, lunging forward. His fist falls like an anvil across the old doctor's face. Bone crunches and blood slicks across the wall.

Doc whimpers.

"It took me twelve months to recover from that cocktail you injected into me," says Drew. "Twelve months I lay there, unable to even take a piss by myself. And then the tests started."

He hits the doc again, this time in the guts. I tighten my grip on the cell door bars. There isn't much meat to the doctor. His years in his cell have weakened him. He doubles over, clutching his stomach, sobbing.

"And they certified me as crazy," continues Drew. "Funny thing is, they put it down to substance abuse having altered my personality."

Blood drips from the doc's chin, a spreading pool of scarlet staining his nightshirt.

"I never meant to hurt you," he whispers. "If I'd known you survived the test, I would have helped."

"Four others died. My brothers-in-arms. You don't get to come back from that."

Drew tugs on the sheet and pulls it free from the doc's ankles.

I sense the nurse's intention. "Get up and fucking fight!" I yell, but the doc has withdrawn and he doesn't hear me.

Drew snatches the sheet and twists it around the doc's throat, tight. Kent's eyes bug as he clutches the cloth. Drew leans in closer.

"It took me forever to find you," he says, flicking spittle. "I escaped from the asylum they locked me up in and then started searching. But it was hard because as far as the real world is concerned, you don't exist."

The doc squeezes out a cough.

"But then I got a job upstairs here in the normal wards. I found your file. It was only too easy to volunteer to help out old Arthur."

Drew loosens the sheet. The doc coughs, desperately sucking air in through his yellowed teeth.

"What? You think I am going to make it that easy?" The sheet falls from Drew's fingers to the cold floor. "Soldier-killers like you don't get to die clean."

Drew digs into his pocket, pulling clear a needle and syringe. Thick yellow liquid sloshes around the cylinder. He removes the cap. The needle tip glints.

"Look familiar?" he says. "It should. And now you're going to die screaming, just like the others."

And that's enough for me. The boy's gone too far. There's no honour in a soldier who would hurt a broken, old man.

Kent has already suffered for his mistakes.

He's more than paid the price.

I smash my fists against the bars of my cell. The metal shudders. I punch again. The bars the doc has built to keep me cornered in his mind fade and once again, like so many times before, I seize control of his body.

Drew notices the change. He steps back as I straighten the doc's shoulders for him.

"You will keep your hands off my doctor," I spit. "He may be a fucked-up bastard, but he is *my*, fucked-up bastard!"

I launch off the bed and curl the doc's hands around Drew's throat. It's his turn to be scared, as I squeeze the breath from him. The boy struggles under me, but while the doc's body hurts, my soldier's will is stronger. I grit my teeth, ignoring the grate of a broken cheekbone. I lean forward to leverage what small weight I have against Drew's neck. Deep in the doc's belly, I sense something bleeding.

The boy bucks unexpectedly and my grip on him slips. I fall to the side, the doc's back colliding with the cold iron legs of the bed. New pain blooms across his shoulder. I use the bed to pull us up. But Kent's body is weak and Drew is younger—faster. His fist connects with the doc's chin, snapping his head back. We stumble, palms falling to the mattress and finding the corner of the journal.

Drew advances, eyes wild, the syringe clutched in his hand.

I grasp the book.

And with every ounce of the doc's remaining strength, I swing and smash the journal into Drew's face. The weight of our words, both mine and Kent's, held sacred in the pages, do their job. Drew stumbles backwards, blood colouring his lips. He slips on the fallen sheet and crashes to the ground.

He lands turned away from the door, features hidden in shadow. He pulls his hand clear of his body. And the shadows and light shift. I grin.

The syringe and needle are imbedded in his side.

The cocktail is in his bloodstream now.

Drew struggles to his feet. He glances my way, horror and fury warring in his gaze. But he says nothing. There is nothing left to be said. The boy heads for the open doorway. Clutching his side, he exits, pulling the door closed behind him. I roar in victory as the lock clicks shut. But then the doc's body slumps.

It's hard to find the strength to straighten the bed before laying him down. But I manage it. As thanks for his years of care, I'll see that the doc is given some measure of dignity. I lay him flat. His breaths come ragged. I touch his stomach. The pain is blinding. Something is broken there.

I retreat from his mind and move back into my own cell. I watch him for a moment, swallowing back guilt. I wish I'd acted sooner. I could have done more for him. But wishes are for fools. All I can offer him now is his privacy and his freedom to die in peace.

I turn and lie down on my own bed. Old habit finds my fingers crawling to my arm. For the first time ever, I find no chips imbedded in my flesh.

I smile.

So with the doc's freedom, comes my own.

In the other room, Kent breathes his last breath.

I glance over. His spirit raises clear of his corpse. Death suits him. He looks younger somehow, or maybe less mad. I'm not sure.

He turns to face his ghosts. At first his translucent form stands apart from them, uncertain. But then they gather him into their circle. They are content, it seems, that their murders have been avenged, and that in being murdered, Kent Rhys is their kin.

The doc turns his attention to me, gaze questioning.

Are you okay?

I sigh, knowing his departure signals mine also. But I'm ready. I raise my hand and salute him. He salutes back, smiling.

Patchwork Reapers

In the desert, against the common smells of sun-blistered sand and rock, the scent of blood stands out. That's how I first find his horse. The Appaloosa, with its head missing, rests laid out in the dust. Bosco, my boss, lies fifty yards further on. He's face up by the edge of the dried creek that runs the length of Skullcap Canyon. His boots, tips worn, point awkwardly to the vast midday sky. Blood seeps from the hole that's been punched clean through his heart.

Damned stubborn idiot.

He knew what we were up against. We went out to find missing longhorns and men, and he saw the same as I did—a gore-soaked plain littered with slaughtered cattle and the bodies of our boys, Billy, Ike and Jonah, alongside them.

He saw how whoever killed them, stole their heads.

But Bosco was anxious. He went ahead alone to warn that new wife his, even though everyone knows she's more than capable of looking after herself.

My horse, Isha, shifts uneasily. Not sure if it's being so near to the body or her response to my own fretfulness. I glance up at the rugged crags that line the ravine. Are Bosco's murderers waiting for me in the cliffs? Lots of places to hide up there—places easy to set up an ambush.

I spit to clear the fear-taste from my mouth. Shit. I didn't ask for any of this. I just came west to drive longhorns for coin.

A rock clatters, breaking the canyon's silence. I twist in the saddle, my heart a knot. I run a hand down my trouser leg. Around me the dry red cliffs bare their teeth.

My trigger finger twitches. Got to keep moving. I won't leave my boss behind though. I slide off Isha. The blood on Bosco's shirt is dark and clotted. I reach in under his arms and lift him to a sitting position. His body has started to stiffen. My mare holds steady as I ease him up to rest belly down across the saddle. We follow the creek bed.

My plan is a simple one. Get back to the ranch, drop Bosco to his widow, pack my bedroll and hightail it the hell out of here. I'm not getting paid enough to stick around.

Ahead a tall, lean shape detaches from an outcrop of rocks. Two others join it.

Bandits?

I suck a breath through gritted teeth. Something about the way they walk isn't right.

These things don't move like men.

The light play changes and their features solidify. Hell and damnation. They look to be some kind of machines, rusted iron arms and hands hanging lax and ready by their sides. Metal legs and torsos too, but they…

Gods. Each one wears a dead man's face—Billy's, Ike's and Jonah's—lips all jerking, eyes blinking unnatural-like.

Bile claws my throat.

The monsters move in perfect unison. Their heavy feet break stones as they approach, an awful crunching like the snapping of bones. Isha screams and rears. Her reins slither free from my grasp. I snatch for the flying ends, but miss.

The last machine-man in the line—the one with Billy's face—lifts its hand, palm facing out and glowing. A terrible whine fills the air followed by a knife of blue-white light from the creature's hand. Isha falls to it, her skull lost in a rain of blood and brains. Her momentum carries her on for two more strides then, along with Bosco, she topples sideways to the ground.

"Isha! NO!" I scream.

Heart pounding, I draw. Bullets spark uselessly off the metal chest plates. My cylinder clicks over, empty.

The machines halt ten paces from me. They blink stickily. The one wearing Ike raises its hand, again with palm alight. The high-pitched whine builds again.

I run.

A blast of heat and light sears past me.

My boots catch in depressions of stone and sink through softer patches of red-yellow sand. I know I'm already dead, but a man in his last moments wants to know he gave his all.

The rock arch that marks the end of the canyon looms ahead. The cliffs past it veer away, bleeding into empty desert. I glance across my shoulder.

Another whine and another shot scores past my ear. I swerve left. Their uncanny footsteps grow louder.

I reckon I can smell the oil in their joints.

Saltbush clutches me as I barrel past. Ahead, an errant gust of wind twists up into a column of dust and then dances away. The vast emptiness calls me on.

Before long my legs and lungs betray me. I collapse to the sand with a grunt. Gravel grazes my palms. I taste sweat on my lips. These are the last, small details of my life.

Will I know it when they take my head?

A gunshot shatters the plain. Good, human-sounding gunfire. The noise ricochets off into the distance and is replaced with the drumming cadence of galloping hooves.

I roll to the side as two horsemen approach huddled low over their mounts. Where the hell did they come from? I cover my head as one of them leaps over me. Amidst dust and falling grass, I see the rider swing a tomahawk. Billy's head sails free, trailing a bunch of cables out from the severed neck.

Decapitated, the mechanical body stops dead.

Two more cuts. Two more heads roll to the grass. Sparks spit from the ends of the severed wires as Ike's and Jonah's mouths open and close for a few moments. A wash of black liquid floods past their lips and then they stop moving.

The lead rider loops back to me, the tomahawk held wide of the mount and the edge dripping black. He lifts his chin and the stark light catches his features.

Except *he* is a *she*. A forty-something-aged woman, eyes and hair dark as pitch, and her skin the colour of warm dusk.

Bosco's wife, Orenda. The half-Cherokee woman he gambled and lost his life for.

"You all right, Clayton?" she asks.

I nod, too exhausted to speak.

"The others?"

I shake my head.

"Bosco?"

"Gone," I croak. "He's back there in the canyon, still tied to what's left of my horse."

No emotion registers at the news of her dead husband. Orenda tips her chin to her offsider—her lean brother, Ahuli, the cowboy who arrived only last week to help with work on the ranch.

Glances pass between them. Ahuli then nods and gallops off in a cloud of dust. Seems he'll be the one to bring the boss home.

Orenda, dressed like a man in trousers, blue neckerchief and a button-up shirt, slithers off her horse. She wipes her axe's edge clean on a tussock of wiry grass and re-holsters it to her saddle. She offers me a waterskin.

The liquid is warm and tastes slightly oily but I'm thankful for her kindness.

"We found…" I begin, but then words fail me.

"I know," says Orenda, saving me from finishing. Ghosts dance in the depths of her eyes. "The house was attacked this morning. We two are all that made it out."

I bite my lip. There were twenty other staff stationed at the ranch.

Ahuli returns, his bay gelding huffing out urgent breaths as he's reined to a stop.

"I found the mount but the boss is gone," he says, his voice as deep as the drum he was named for. His horse sidles and he pulls him straight. "Their tracks head back down the canyon."

"We'll follow them," says Orenda.

"Are you serious?" I clench my fists. "You've seen what those *things* will do to us."

"I'll not leave my husband with them."

"But he's dead!"

Orenda frowns. The lines running from her nose to her mouth deepen. "To believe that means you don't know *all* they are capable of."

"And how would you know?" I ask.

She cocks her head for a moment. Her lips twitch. "Because I listened to the stories my mother told me. I know the truth of what dwells out here."

"And what's that?"

"Unnatural deaths," she replies.

***

The shots start as soon as we pass back under the rock arch. The cliffs ignite into a hailstorm of the machine-men's blue-white firepower. There are at least a hundred of them, hiding like rats in the rocks. The sizzle of their weapons and the creak of their metal limbs sets my teeth on edge.

Ahuli's horse is the first to fall, the gelding's scream cut short as he's mown down. Orenda's buckskin dies next. As her mare drops, we leap clear of the shared saddle and tumble to the sand. I scuttle for shelter behind the closest boulder.

Dodging blasts, Orenda skids over to Ahuli. Grasping the back of his shirt, she drags him to safety. Her brother falls in beside me with a thump, hat missing, hair awry and his Winchester rifle held close to his chest. He rolls over and levels the gun against the top of the boulder and begins to fire. Orenda covers him from the opposite side.

With my own pistol useless, I grab the one tucked into Ahuli's belt. He nods his approval. Together we fire into the approaching enemy, hoping to score the lucky shots that will send them all packing to hell.

The gunfight lasts all of two minutes.

The machines circle us without losing even one of their number—an unholy army gleaming dull in the drifting dust of battle and the dying light. Half of them wear human heads, and others wear human limbs—an arm here, a leg there—a profane blend of flesh and machine. For a moment the creatures remain motionless, then they swivel and step back, creating a corridor.

"Why have they stopped?" I whisper.

"Watch," says Orenda. "Their *didanawisgi* approaches."

I recognise the Cherokee word. *Medicine man.*

A shuffling shape moves from the back of the assembled warriors. A wizened old man appears, bent over a walking stick of gnarled brown wood. At his throat is a thin red welt—a horizontal, knotted scar. I see the same at the exposed flesh on his wrists. His hands are different colours. On one the skin is black and the other is white. His face is different again, an olive tone.

"Put down your weapons," says the Patchwork Man, his voice holding a curious clicking quality. He lifts his head, revealing two different-coloured eyes— one blue, one brown.

I aim my pistol at his heart. "We've come for the body of our friend. Hand it over and we'll be leavin' without further conflict."

"There is no conflict here. Only survival," says the man, tipping his chin toward the closest machine.

It turns. The creature wears Bosco's face.

***

With hands tied behind our backs, we are taken south and into the night. Skullcap Canyon lies far behind us while ahead a mesa rises; a great black shadow against the clear, night desert sky.

Jonah, Billy and Ike, heads now restored to their mechanical bodies, guard us as we march. I try and ignore the Bosco machine that also keeps pace with us. It keeps turning to glance at Orenda and mutters unintelligible words. The clouded eyes of my dead friend seem to beseech his bride, asking her to love him still.

But she pays no heed to him. Back straight, chin up and eyes forward, Orenda walks on.

The mesa's steep sides soon tower overhead. At ground level, the rock face is split by a large vertical crack. A faint humming sound emits from the crevice.

The Patchwork Man slows. He taps his walking stick against the ground and utters a series of clicks. The humming stops and the rock splits to reveal a corridor lit by a distant spill of light. We are led across the threshold. I draw one last breath of clean air before the dreadful door slides closed behind us.

The pathway beyond is short and opens out into a large cavern. Within, the ceiling is concealed by shadow and distance, lost as it is to the heart of the mesa. The area is flooded with an unfamiliar white light. It holds none of the warmth of a lamp or an open fire. Tarnished silver tables lined up in neat rows fill the floor, each with a square metal box connected to the far end. Some hold machine-men lying prone, the rest are filled with half-mutilated human corpses—the staff from the ranch house. I clench my teeth. None of those good people deserved an end like this.

I turn from the gruesome display, searching for an escape. The place is a fortress, heavy and well-fortified. Everything's metal and wires and machines painted over with a ramshackle patina of dust and ancient rust.

There is no way out.

Next to me, Ahuli takes a sharp breath. His usually dusky face is pale. I follow his gaze to a pile of weathered sticks stacked up high against the far cavern wall.

No. Not sticks…

Bones—both animal and human.

I reckon my face turns the colour of Ahuli's.

"We gotta get out of here," I whisper.

He nods.

The Patchwork Man pauses at the centre of the cavern. He turns and the harsh light of the room reveals his skin to be blotched in shades of palest blue and green.

"Welcome," he says.

Welcome? I bunch my fists. "Killin' our folk and haulin' us to this crazy-ass tomb ain't no kind of welcome!"

The old man looks confused for a moment. His mismatched gaze turns to Orenda.

"You haven't told them?" he asks.

She shrugs. "They would not have come if I had."

"What are you talking about, sister?" asks Ahuli, disbelief etching his tone.

"The old stories," Orenda replies. "The Reapers are real."

Ahuli's eyes widen. "It can't be," he whispers.

"It is," she says.

"What in damnation are Reapers?" I ask, not really sure I want the answer.

"Myths. Monsters," says Ahuli, eyes still fixed to his sister. "Desert dwellers who came before men were even a seed of a thought on this land."

"I don't care how long they've been here," I say. "Why do they wanna kill us?"

"Not kill," says Orenda. "We only wish to survive."

"We?" I ask.

She undoes her neckerchief and drops it to the ground. A thin white scar circles the base of her neck and another runs down to disappear between her breasts.

Ahuli steps back, disgusted.

"Why are you not pleased, brother?" asks Orenda.

"Pleased? You've become a monster!"

The Patchwork Man shakes his head. "No. She is a gift. She has saved us."

"Your kind should not be saved," whispers Ahuli.

I've had enough of this. I don't like feeling afraid. "What are you and what the hell do you want from us?" I ask.

The Patchwork Man blinks. "We are worker droids left here thousands of years ago by masters who, when finished seeding life on this planet, abandoned us." He points to the other machines standing behind us. "Our original parts are failing," he continues. "We have been forced to survive on blended metal and flesh—flesh that always rots away."

The Bosco machine gurgles a quiet cry.

"You don't look like you've got any issues," I say.

The Patchwork Man holds up his different-coloured hands. "I have only perfected my new body recently," he says, "with a new modification process I resolved on this female human."

Orenda remains eerily still.

The old man catches me staring at her.

"You are wondering for how long she has deceived you?" he asks, voice sly.

"Thought did cross my mind," I say.

"We captured her two months ago." The old man smiles and I glimpse copper teeth behind his greenish lips. "I successfully transplanted her skin casing and various critical organs onto one of my own people's exoskeletons. Then we sent her out to gather others that could be used for our purpose."

"My sister has been dead for two months?" Ahuli's voice cracks like a bullet through glass.

"Dead? No," says the Patchwork Man. "The machine at her core has control of the body and its programming dominates the flesh-mind processes, but she still maintains her awareness behind that. That is our gift for the sacrifice of her body to our cause."

Gift? Orenda is still alive in there somewhere?

A butterfly trapped in a spider's web.

Suddenly the pain I saw in her eyes earlier takes on new meaning.

"You have violated my sister!" screams Ahuli. He launches, locking his broad hands around the old man's throat.

With a swing that seems all too easy, the Patchwork Man sends Orenda's brother flying. He lands heavily against a table. Bone crunches and he howls, clutching his chest. Bright blood dribbles suddenly down his chin.

The Patchwork Man's eyes glow white for a moment as a thin beam of light runs from them to scan over Ahuli's body. The old man's features ripple into anger.

"Your critical organs are damaged. You are of no value now!"

He nods to Orenda and the tall woman-made-machine stalks over to her brother.

"Orenda," pleads Ahuli.

Without hesitation she tears his head free from his shoulders.

The machine within made her do it. The tears streaking her cheeks betray the truth of that fact, even as her mouth remains cold and resolute.

A different machine-man, one who's rusted limbs screech with every step, strides over and takes possession of the grisly prize.

"Take its arms and legs for yourself too," says the Patchwork Man irritably.

The creature nods and complies. It carries Ahuli's parts to a table and lays them out. Clear tubes, with a life of their own, snake out of the box at the table's end and imbed themselves into what remains of Ahuli's neck and severed limbs. A black liquid is pumped through them. The head reanimates, lax lips beginning to move and eyes blinking in rapid succession. Ahuli's disconnected limbs shudder also, fingers and toes twitching.

The machine-man detaches its degenerated parts. More cables snake from within its body's open connective points and slither through the raw, bloodied ends to link with fleshy tendons. The last part replaced is Ahuli's head, fitted to the metal neck socket, his eyes mirror abject horror.

My stomach surges. My palms turn sweaty. Orenda grabs me by the shoulder.

"This way," she says.

Her grip is iron.

I have no choice but to go where she leads.

We pass what's left of Ahuli's body. The spreading pool of his blood is too scarlet against the red rock floor. If what the Patchwork Man says is right, eventually, fitted to that machine, Ahuli will die. Right now, all-the-way-dead is better sounding than becoming trapped in a machine's skin overcoat.

We stop at an empty table. When encouraged to lie down I twist and drop my shoulder into Orenda's chest. Her skin gives but beneath I meet a wall of iron. I grunt and fall back against the table.

Orenda lifts her hand, balled into a fist but the old man stops her.

"Do not damage it," he says. "We need the body whole."

Orenda complies. She steps back and to one side.

"Get on the table," says the Patchwork Man.

"No."

"It was not a request."

"I didn't take it as one."

"I am gifting you immortality."

I shake my head. "It's slavery."

The old man frowns. He lifts his walking stick and for the first time I notice the back length of it is honed and sharpened to a knife's keen edge.

"We will do what we must to survive," he says.

"Go to hell," I snarl.

The Patchwork Man leans in.

I don't feel the slice across my neck as his blade passes.

But I do taste the blood in my mouth.

ALL WHO ARE WARRIORS

T hey never answer, but I often curse the Keres—
those heartless spirits, those goddesses of death.
I tell them they are dogs. As a child, gifted with birth-
born magic to behold the uncanny, I witnessed their
savagery—witnessed them drinking the blood of my
kin as they were slaughtered at the hands of Pecheneg
raiders. Again, years later, my husband, a cavalry
warrior and pride of Constantinople, fell to those
same spirits—one of many to perish on the plains of
Anatolia. With his death and debts amounted I, once a
noblewoman, am now a palace slave. Even with my
gifts, I couldn't save my loved ones, couldn't hold my
position. The Keres took everything from me.

But I've not given up hope for redemption.

Today the palace corridors bustle with servants,
nobility and nervous activity. I balance my mistress's
breakfast platter in the crook of my elbow. The smell

of fresh oranges and dates curls up and my stomach growls, my breakfast of bread and honey not enough to satisfy. I turn my attention to the crowd. Gossip rides thick in the air—words soar from lips with wings.

"Did you hear, Serina?" snickers Senator Thalis's wife to her sister. "The captain of the Varangian Guard has been accused of treason. The hearing is to be held in the Hippodrome today."

"Erik Thorbjornsson? What a waste. He's a handsome devil."

"Certainly. Enough to make any married woman swoon."

Serina giggles. "Enough to make *this* married woman swoon. My husband is impotent. Perhaps I should petition the emperor to gift me Erik?"

"No, sister. Those northern men worship savage gods. Safer to find a plaything that won't disembowel you."

The women pass and I bite my lip. The news of Erik's fall from favour is not unexpected. Rumours have abounded for days, whispered conversations between the chambermaids who claim that Erik succumbed to Grand Princess Helene's desires for him. The emperor's hired Varangian mercenary's liaison with the princess is an act of treason, even if done with consent. The princess, fearing her father's wrath, has tried to save herself by claiming she was forced.

Emperor Hector must be furious. He's lost a valuable tool in bargaining with foreign kings—for what ruler would marry a sullied princess?

As if my grim thoughts have the power to summon dark omens, three Keres appear in the corridor ahead. When not in the throes of bloodlust, they move serenely. Their winged, translucent forms are, as always, cast in shades of black and white, except for their lips and claws, which are brutal scrawls of scarlet. My heart sinks: they only come when someone is about to die.

I adjust the platter.

"Dogs," I mutter, teeth clenched.

The Keres halt and turn, pinning their savage gazes on me. Bloody tears mar each of the death spirits' pallid faces. I stumble, almost colliding with another woman who curses me irritably. The goddesses have never acknowledged me before, and never have I seen them weep.

"We come unwilling, bidden by dark curses," they say in unison, voices like snakeskin over gravel. "Save the condemned man if you wish for he is not ours to take. His own gods will revolt if we are forced to do so."

The man? Save Erik?

The Keres then turn and fade into the crowd. I draw an unsettled breath.

My thoughts race but I maintain equilibrium by focusing on the everyday details of the morning—the colour of the sunlight streaming in through the windows and the way the halls bustle with white-clad slaves rushing in service to their masters.

Save the man.

I owe the Keres nothing, but I've no desire to meet any northern gods either. My resolve galvanises. Where I couldn't save my own family, maybe I can save this foreign man.

I hold my head down and ears open. The corridor reverberates with varied conversations and any scrap of gossip may aid me. Small, unimportant facts are gleaned: a measure of mandrake root has been stolen from the royal physician's stores and the princess has been ill these past five mornings, requesting ginger tea. But on the lips of most is the single question—

Will the Varangian captain survive the day?

I need to ensure I'm on the royal dais, attending my mistress, Anna for the hearing. She is a minor cousin to Emperor Hector and her presence has been requested. From there I will observe the proceedings and look for an opportunity. As I approach the apartments, the sound of Anna's shrill voice pierces the heavy timber door.

"Useless shrew! The silk skirts, not the linen!" The sound of an entitled hand slapping a young slave's cheek filters through the wood. "Now, get them!"

I shake my head, feeling for the attendant. Being Anna's handmaiden is a unique punishment. The woman is bitter in nature and though she wields no true power in the court, she holds the respect of the emperor and that makes her dangerous. One word from her lips and a slave's head can roll.

I enter the suite. The room is full of light, streaming in from the open doors leading to a balcony that overlooks the gardens. Anna, her pitch-dark tresses piled high in elaborate fashion, simpers in front of a mirror standing central to the room. The chambermaid, Dimitria, her cheek imprinted with a red handprint, stands to one side, carefully holding the skirts requested. She holds her mouth pinched, biting back tears.

Anna lifts her chin and spies the food platter. "What took you so long, Ekaterina? I wish for you to attend me today and I must be seated closest to the princess before the other cousins arrive."

Luck is on my side.

"Of course, Mistress," I reply. "The chefs send their apologies. They were overwhelmed this morning." I place the food on the table next to a collection of oddities—a small, red silk bag, a bunch of dried plant roots, and a mortar and pestle.

Anna swishes across the room, her sandals whispering over the pale marble floors. She arranges herself on the seat and leans forward. She selects a plump olive from the platter and pops it into her mouth. Then she reaches for the mortar and spoons from it a small amount of dark powder into the silk bag. The heavy red-apple scent of mandrake circles me.

I frown. Anna glances up and smiles, teeth white like a shark's. "A poesy to help with the smell should the emperor choose to disembowel our dear Captain Thorbjornsson."

Anna looks thrilled by the idea.

But then again, Erik did leave her bed in favour of the grand princess's.

***

The Hippodrome is filled to bursting. The morning sun beats bright over the empty track, but above it, each terrace overflows with a raucous, multi-coloured crowd. Still my ears are open, looking for opportunity. I sift and sort the nearest conversations, finding nothing of value. My past has distilled into this one moment—one moment in which my gift can make a difference, even if it's just for a man with no ties to my own gods.

I extend my awareness outwards, gauging the mood of the crowd. The disposition of the citizens seems varied. Some scream with expectation, here to witness the spectacle of a man condemned. Others sit quietly, pensive and nervous, as they watch the grim-faced Varangian Guard standing at attention at the base of the dais. The silent are the shrewd. For like them, I recognise the danger that hovers.

Will Erik's loyal men react with violence when their captain is condemned to death?

I stand slightly behind Anna's chair. She has, as she wanted, secured the closest to the grand princess's throne. The princess herself sits next to her father, her face pale as marble and dark gaze distant. The emperor lounges in his royal robes, his heavy brow furrowed like a thundercloud. The way his fingers clench his seat's armrest shows his desire to be done here. He has already made his decision. This hearing is only to show the people that he is a good and fair ruler—a point of considerable importance to him, I hear.

The crowd shifts, signalling Erik's approach into the ring.

I can't help but recall the first time I saw him, a day three years past, when he rode ahead of his men into the capitol. He towered sitting astride a great barrel-chested stallion, an animal that seemed as if it would breathe fire if it could. On that bright morning, his long, gold hair shone like a beacon in the sun, his new red cloak, emblazoned with the dragon insignia of the emperor's Varangian Guard, had gleamed ruby against the age-worn stone that is the foundation of Constantinople. Without doubt, Erik Thorbjornsson presented as a lion amongst men.

But today he rides no horse. Erik is naked and bound, flanked by prison guards. The scarlet he wears is not a cloak, but blood dripping from beard to broad chest. The guards herd him to the base of the dais and kick the backs of his knees to set him upon the ground.

By the gods, the man has grace, even when falling.

I glance at Erik's kinsmen. Others might miss the minute shifting of their feet and clenching of their fists. They are unhappy. I swallow.

"Emperor Hector," calls one of the guards. He bows his head and pounds a fist to his breastplate. "Erik Thorbjornsson, the accused."

Hector waves an imperious hand. The guards step back, swords drawn. Even with him bound, they fear their prisoner.

"Cowards," snaps Erik, sonorous voice deep as a well. He glances up at the emperor. "And so is the man who rules them."

Hector sneers. "You are the dog here."

Erik snarls, his teeth bloodied behind his broken lips. He ignores the emperor's comment and instead trains those eyes of his—glacial blue like the ice from his homeland—unfailingly on Helene.

"Are you satisfied?" he asks. "Do these chains absolve you?"

The princess's attention remains distant and fixed to the crowd.

"Silence," demands Hector. "You are accused of treason," states the emperor, voice pitched to cross the Hippodrome.

Erik spits blood, scarlet against the bright sand. He squints against the midday light. "Your daughter knows the truth. My honour is intact."

Helene's gaze drops.

Hector raises his hand again. "Traitors have no honour. Have you no other argument to defend yourself, Varangian?"

"I'll not lie if that is what you are asking for."

"You will die today," says Hector.

"I do not fear death."

The emperor's chin lifts. "This I know. Just as I know the manner in which you die is of interest to your own gods."

"My gods will not forsake me."

The air ripples around Erik. I blink. The Keres, smelling imminent blood, have appeared. They gather at his back, all still weeping.

Save him...

Erik, again, addresses Helene.

"Princess," growls the Northman, "in my country, women are warriors. And so are you. There's no shame in our union—in you having taken what you want."

The princess swallows. Her father grasps her arm. She winces and then clasps her hands tightly in her lap. She looks away.

The emperor's brown-black eyes glitter with satisfaction. "Erik Thorbjornsson, foreigner in our country," he calls out. "For your crime, I should have molten lead poured down your throat and your limbs severed. But our religion is not yours, so something *other* will be your punishment."

Erik's gaze thins. Mutters break out amongst his men. Light sparks off the edges of the great axes strapped to their backs.

"Give me a sword and let me die in battle, Emperor. You owe me that for my service to your country."

The emperor stands in a violent billow of robes. Even at full height he is a small man. "I AM this country and I owe you nothing." He leans in. His voice lowers so only those closest can hear. "For ruining my daughter, I'll pass no sentence allowing you to enter the halls of your Valhalla."

The emperor snaps a ringed finger. At the signal Anna stands. My confusion turns to sudden horror. For my mistress's face is changed, not only ugly with delight, but also it crawls as if shadows seethe behind her skin. She unknots the red silk bag from her belt and crumples it into her palm. She begins to mutter, words that hold sharp edges and embers.

Dark curses…

My gift allows me to see all. I step back as fiery symbols appear, scorching the air around me, and circle to rest upon the emperor's head and drape in chains around Erik's broad shoulders. A bitter smell comes from the herbs smouldering in the silk bag.

The Keres shudder and their eyes turn white. Their voices rise to a painful cry as their lips peel back to reveal vampiric teeth. They claw at their temples and tear their hair, but Anna's foul magic binds them like moths to flame. The symbols circle the spirits and fill their mouths until the three vomit fire across their breasts. Then they fall still.

Anna crumbles the silk bag, now turned to ashes, and twists her hand. The air around the Keres shivers as they are summoned to the physical plane.

The crowd gasp in shock. All eyes now see what I have spent a lifetime fearing—the terrifying true faces of death.

"They are yours to command, Emperor," says Anna.

"Kill him!" cries Hector.

The Keres respond, claws and fangs extended. The three fall upon Erik to feed on his exposed neck.

The Varangian captain convulses. His eyes roll back and he slumps backward.

Save the man...

I throw my arm across Anna's neck and securing a chokehold, I squeeze. She chokes, clawing the back of my arm. My mind roars like a tempest fed by fear and anger, and I barely notice the emperor screaming for his guards, Helene weeping, or the crowd surging to their feet and cheering.

I've never killed before—adrenaline and instinct guide me. I grit my teeth and will power into my grip but Anna twists and drops her elbow into my belly. Coughing, I double over with pain, only just able to hold my grip. Breaths ragged, I drag her down with me and on my knees I rally. I grasp my opposite wrist, pulling my forearm tighter across her throat. I growl and reel backwards. She gurgles. Her struggles slow then stop. Dead, she slumps to the ground.

"Restrain the slave!" screeches the emperor.

I release Anna and reel back, hands held up.

Hector howls his rage, spittle landing on my cheek. The reality of my predicament crashes around me. I've just murdered the emperor's favourite cousin.

I haven't saved Erik. I'll die alongside him.

The guard's battle-hardened hands are coarse against my skin. They drag me roughly upright, tearing the shoulder of my slip.

"Keres!" screams Hector.

Bound to Hector, the three spirits halt their frenzied feeding to answer his call. Erik slouches as they release him and rise into the air. They land wordlessly before me—black and white figures, chins slick with the captain's blood. Their nostrils flare, the promise of my own death circling in their eyes.

I try to not fear what's next.

"Father. Stop. What is happening?"

The princess straightens. She's no longer weeping but blinks as if waking from a sudden dream. She glances at Anna's fallen form and back at her father. Realisation dawns across her young face like a rising sun. Then her brows lower and defiance builds in her gaze, regal and terrifying to witness.

"You ordered your witch cousin to spell away my free will, my heart and conscience?"

Hector swivels on his heel. "Silence. I did what I must to hide your transgressions!"

"You had no right, Father."

"I am ruler of this empire."

"And I am your heir," says Helene. "I'll not let you kill the man I love nor the slave who would save him." Her hands flutter to her belly, her voice hardens. "Erik is father to your grandchild. Tell me, what other soldier in your armies has more cause to defend our family?"

Erik raises his head. His bloodied throat is a slash of colour against the pale of his face. "You are with child?"

The emperor's eyes bulge. His cheeks bunch as he chews unspoken words like bile. Finally he points to Helene. "Keres. Take her too."

"Father! What are you doing?"

"NO!" yells Erik.

The three spirits advance. They growl with anticipation.

Don't just save the man. Save them all...

I've known the Keres my entire life.

They have consumed the blood of my family.

And that forges connection.

With a cry, I twist free of the guards and lunge between the princess and the Keres. The spirits pause scenting my bloodline, a known and familiar elixir to them, and as I hoped, it is the greater draw.

I cry out as their teeth find me, hot pins against the tender skin of my throat. They pierce my flesh and savage a hole into my artery. A sudden hot rush of blood slicks my chest.

I hold my arms wide and let them feed. I let them feed to save an innocent man. I let them feed to defend a princess in love and a child not yet born.

Then when I am drained, the Keres stop drinking. They pull back suddenly, their forms returned to translucent spirits, their eyes clear.

The magic in my blood has done its work.

***

The flagstones are cold against my cheek and the air trembles with activity. Stubbornness alone keeps me lucid and breathing. I blink and flashpoint images of a raging battle register—the crowd fleeing as the Varangian Guard swarms the Hippodrome, great axes swinging—palace guards cut down and left to bleed on sand tossed and marred.

On the dais a smaller conflict ensues, with the outcome weightier. Erik, sword in hand, advances on the emperor who huddles fearfully against his seat. Around him lie the bodies of his guard, their prowess no match for the Varangian warrior's skill. Overhead the Keres soar, holding a pattern in the sky, waiting to feed.

"You can't kill me!" screeches Hector.

The princess stands grey-faced but resolute. She presses her hand to her small belly. "Finish it, Erik," she commands.

I don't witness the deathblow, but see the Keres dip their wings. They land with claws extended and drag Hector's screaming soul from his body. The sound echoes in my head as they carry him past me on their way to the pits of Tarturus.

It's ended. A bitter victory. Numb, I roll to my back. I fix my gaze to midday-blue arc of sky. Faces hover in and out of view, ladies of the court, the grand princess and her bloodied, bare-chested Varangian mate.

Erik kneels at my side.

"You are brave," he says.

I glance at him and see the truth of my death written in his eyes.

"I'm afraid," I whisper.

"Do not fear dying," says Erik softly. "For a death earned in battle, you'll be welcomed in Valhalla."

"But your gods won't know me."

"It matters not." Erik places his broad hand on my brow. "Odin embraces all who are warriors."

Acknowledgments

My sincere thanks go to the various editors who worked with me on the previously published stories in this collection. Thanks also to Lauren and Geneve, my exceptional Inklings! To Jan-Andrew, thank you for the coffee chats, for loving my stories and for always encouraging me to do more. And to my parents, your support and feedback mean the world to me.

And, as always, my family. Darren, Piper and Dakota; you are my sunshine on rainy days.

REFERENCES

'Monstrous In Nature' first appeared in the anthology, *The Zookeeper's Tales of Interstellar Oddities,* CAT Press, March 2020

'Passenger' previously titled 'Alex Logan' first appeared in the anthology, *Passenger 13*, Black Hare Press, May 2020

'These Many Dead Men' previously titled 'Kent Rhys' first appeared in the anthology, *Disturbed*, Black Ink Fiction, October 2021

'Dread Circus' first appeared in the anthology, *That is Too Wrong: An Anthology of Offbeat Horror Vol II,* Black Hart Publishing, August 2022

'Universe, Devoured' first appeared in the magazine, *Midnight Echo Issue 17,* Australian Horror Writers Association, August 2022

'Patchwork Reapers' first appeared in the anthology *SNAFU: Dead or Alive*, Cohesion Press, October 2022

About the Author

Pamela Jeffs is a speculative fiction author living in Queensland, Australia with her husband and two daughters. Her work has been published previously in various magazines and anthologies, both nationally and internationally, and has been shortlisted for numerous Australian Aurealis and Ditmar Awards.

Prior to pursuing her passion for writing, Pamela's background was in interior and exhibition design. This allowed her to collaborate with a multitude of talented artists and designers across a number of artistic platforms.

Precarious Waters is her sixth collection and features both new and previously published work.

To discover more books by Pamela Jeffs and be notified of new releases, deals and specials, visit and subscribe at:

www.pamelajeffs.com
Twitter: @Pamela_Jeffs
Facebook: @pamelajeffsauthor
Bluesky: @pamelajeffs.bsky.social

OTHER TITLES

Discover other titles by Pamela Jeffs at:
www.pamelajeffs.com

Including:

Collections
Red Hour and Other Strange Tales
Saloons & Stardust: A Collection
Five Dragons
The Terralight Collection
The Seasonals

Co-Authored Anthologies
The Zookeeper's Tales of Interstellar Oddities

Children's Fiction
Turtle Island

If you enjoyed this book, please go to Goodreads
and/or Amazon and leave a review. It helps!
Thank you.

www.ingramcontent.com/pod-product-compliance
Lightning Source LLC
Chambersburg PA
CBHW020523120726
47904CB00003B/950